MURDER IN THE GOLDILOCKS ZONE

PAULA BERNSTEIN

M&Z PRESS

PRAISE FOR PAULA BERNSTEIN

"A whip-smart, page turner, with great appeal for academics, scientists, and anyone who has ever wondered about the world of academic astronomy, and so timely, as the 2019 Nobel Prize for Physics was given for the discovery of extrasolar planets."

BEN ZUCKERMAN PHD, PROFESSOR OF
PHYSICS AND ASTRONOMY, UCLA

"Conflict is key in any good story, and here you have a homicide detective working a case involving a pregnant patient in his fiancé's obstetrical practice. Talk about relationship challenges! Added to this is a top caliber mystery that utilizes the author's medical background and will make us pay more attention to what's in our coffee cups!"

LAURIE STEVENS, AUTHOR OF THE GABRIEL
MCRAY SUSPENSE SERIES

For my wonderful husband Uri, who shares my passion for astronomy.

INTRODUCTION

I admit it. I'm an astronomy junkie. I've been fascinated by astronomy since I was a small child and memorized the names and characteristics of all the planets. In an alternate timeline, I might have chosen to study the birth of stars instead of babies. Alas, I got bored in Physics during classical mechanics, so I headed for Chemistry instead. But in order to hedge my bets, I married a physicist.

Over the years, the two of us have taken lots of astronomy courses and attended many symposia to keep up with current astronomical events. We also regularly pick the brains of our astronomer friends. We tried to groom our daughter to be an astrophysicist, but she majored in sociology instead. Some children just insist on having minds of their own.

Of all the developments in astronomy, I've been most fascinated by the search for extrasolar planets. I'd always believed they were there in great numbers, and I have no doubt that eventually we will find habitable ones. I thought I'd share my passion with my readers in this latest Hannah Kline novel. Enjoy.

PROLOGUE

I T WAS JUST SHORT OF SIX IN THE MORNING WHEN THE telephone rang in the bedroom of Professor and Mrs. George Taylor. George rolled over and groaned, pulling the down comforter over his head. It had to be a wrong number. No one ever called them at this hour. Barbara Taylor jerked awake, reaching for the receiver.

"Hello," she said, pushing herself up and leaning against the headboard. "Yes, he is. Who's calling?" Her eyes widened. "Hold for just a moment and I'll get him."

Shaking her head in disbelief, she put the call on hold and shoved her husband roughly, pulling the duvet off his hidden head.

"George, wake up. It's for you, someone from Sweden. He said he was from the Nobel committee."

George sat up like a shot. At last. He was the chairman of the Physics and Astronomy department at the University of California Technological Institute. He'd been on the short list for the Nobel for years now, enduring disappointment after disappointment as his forty-year contribution to elementary particle physics was passed over. It was about time.

"George Taylor here," he said.

"Dr. Taylor, I apologize for phoning so early on a Saturday morning. My name is Sven Pierrson, from the Nobel Prize committee in Stockholm. We've been trying to reach your colleague, Dr. Edwin Larramore, but we don't have a home number. And of course, on a Saturday, no one is answering the phone in the Astronomy offices at your institution. You'll be delighted to know that Dr. Larramore has been awarded the Nobel for his recent spectacular discovery. Your department must be very proud to have yet another, distinguished winner."

George swallowed, trying to restrain his fury. A Nobel Prize for that arrogant, narcissistic asshole. Nothing could have ruined his day faster.

"If you'll hold just a moment, I'll check my cell phone. I'm sure I have both his home number and his mobile listed."

Barbara was looking at him strangely, but she waited until he'd completed the call before asking him what was wrong.

"It's Larramore. They're giving that bastard the Nobel." His face was livid with rage.

"Oh, darling," said Barbara, "I am so sorry."

Carolyn Larramore poured herself a cup of cinnamon apple herbal tea and sat down with the morning's Los Angeles Times. It was one of her weekend rituals. She liked getting up early and having an hour to herself, before Edwin came in demanding breakfast and announcing his plans for their weekend. Fortunately, today, Edwin had already left for his office, so her day would be peaceful. He had just received the telescope data download from his latest observational project and couldn't wait until Monday to look at it. Perhaps she'd go to the Farmer's Market.

When the phone rang, she grabbed it. "Is this some kind of a practical joke?" she said, upon hearing the caller's words. "Edwin's won the Nobel? Really?"

"It's no joke, Mrs. Larramore. Your husband's made an extraordinary contribution to science. May I speak to him, please?"

"He's not here," Carolyn said. "He left early for his office. I can give you his mobile number and private line."

When she hung up, she took a deep breath. She supposed she should be happy to be married to a Nobel Prize-winning scientist, but all she could think of was that this would be the final straw. Edwin was already so full of himself, this last award would make him intolerable. She had seriously considered leaving him a few months ago. Then, she'd discovered she was pregnant. To soothe herself, she stroked her bulging belly and focused on the baby's movements. Carolyn had always wanted a child, but as the pregnancy progressed, she became less and less certain that she could stand living with its father.

Professor Edwin Larramore turned on his computer, gave a satisfied smile, and closed the door to his office. Astronomy had become so much easier. He remembered his graduate student days and the all night observing sessions. At least telescope observations could now be done remotely. No more driving up to the top of some volcano, acclimatizing for a night to get used to the altitude, and putting up with the freezing cold and the dreadful cafeteria food. All he had to do now was to write a proposal, get it funded and be assigned his telescope time. Then, some technician would program his requested observations and make his data available to download. He couldn't wait to see it, but first, some coffee.

Larramore was a purist when it came to his coffee. None of that department swill for his refined taste buds. He preferred Peet's espresso, or when he could get it, beans from one of the boutique coffee roasters. He kept a small refrigerator in his office for soy milk and his own high-tech espresso machine. He noted that he was almost out of coffee, as he measured two scoops carefully into the filter. He added bottled water, and while the espresso was dripping, he steamed a quarter-cup of soy milk to a perfect foam. He liked it the consistency of shaving cream. He poured the coffee and the milk into his special mug and took it to his desk, settling comfortably into his executive chair. Nothing like that first morning hit of caffeine.

____

I LOVE SATURDAY MORNING. IT'S MY FIRST OPPORTUNITY all week to sleep in past my usual 6:30 AM alarm. Sometimes, I even stay in bed until 8:00. I opened my eyes, rolled over and put my head on my fiancé, Daniel's, shoulder. He wasn't quite awake yet, but he put his arm around me and snuggled. The other three members of our household are my six-year-old daughter, Zoe, who enjoys sleeping in even more than I do, and our felines, Mittens and Ginger. At Zoe's request, the cats sleep in her room, as a result of which, my slumbers are not disturbed when they decide it is time for the staff to prepare breakfast. I looked at my watch and decided that 8:45 was beyond the point of self-indulgence, especially since we were meeting our realtor this morning to begin the process of house hunting. I disengaged from Daniel and headed for the shower.

Daniel had recently succeeded in selling his charming Venice bungalow for an absurdly inflated price, so we now had a hefty down payment to supplement the funds I had from my late husband, Ben's, trust fund. I was waiting until we found a suitable house before putting my Brentwood condominium on the market. I had no illusions about the ease of finding the perfect home on the Westside of Los Angeles.

Daniel's realtor had been his ex-wife. She had offered to help us find our nest, and would no doubt have been pleased to get the listing for my condominium, but happy as I was that she and Daniel had a cordial relationship, house hunting with her felt too close for comfort. Daniel had politely declined her offer without any prompting from me, which convinced me once again that I'd selected the right guy. Plus, he had good taste in jewelry. I loved my antique emerald engagement ring.

Our new realtor was Jacqueline Cantor, a pleasant lady in her sixties, who had helped my practice partner and her husband to find their home. She was low key, and according to my partner, smart enough not to suggest that every house we saw was perfect for us.

I put on a pair of gray wool pants and a fuzzy black sweater, brushed out my long red hair, and applied some blush and lipstick. On my way downstairs to the kitchen, I gently woke Daniel and told him coffee would be ready in a few minutes.

To my surprise, Zoe was actually up and playing with the cats on the kitchen floor. I got out a can of tuna and kidney, filled the cat water bowl, and started the coffee. Zoe wanted Honey Nut Cheerios for breakfast and I wanted scrambled eggs with cheddar cheese, so I whisked up some eggs and waited for Daniel to come downstairs.

"Good morning, everyone," he said.

Zoe smiled. Mittens and Ginger ignored him, and I kissed his cheek and handed him a mug with black coffee. I never understood how he could manage to look so sexy in the morning. Daniel was well over six feet tall. His craggy face, with its deep blue eyes, smiled at me. His dark hair, with hints of gray, was still wet from the shower. He was wearing jeans and a long-sleeved black T-shirt that clung to his well muscled chest. All in all, an enticing sight across the breakfast table.

"Mommy, why can't I go with you to look for houses?" Zoe asked.

"Not today, sweetheart. You have a playdate. But I promise that if we find anything we are seriously considering, we'll take you with us, so you can decide if you like it."

"I don't want to be too far away from my school and my friends," she said.

"Don't worry," I said. "I don't want to be too far away from my hospital and my friends either."

I had given the realtor strict instructions about where I was willing to move. Being an obstetrician, I do an unfortunate amount of driving in the middle of the night, and I didn't want to be very far from Labor and Delivery. I'd taken a map and a compass and drawn a twenty-minute circle around Memorial, and eliminated the eastern half, since Daniel, a detective with the LAPD, also worked on the Westside. This left us with the most expensive real estate prices in town, so I knew our search would be challenging.

I filled two plates with scrambled eggs and sat down at the table. Two minutes later, Daniel's cell phone rang. The minute I saw his face, I knew I was going to be house hunting by myself.

"What is it?" I asked, after he hung up.

"A suspicious death over at UCTI, the Technological Institute. Some astronomer was found dead at his desk by one of his graduate students. Brenda took the call. I need to get over there and assess the situation. I'm sorry Hannah."

I shrugged. "If we only made plans on weekends, when neither of us is on call, we'd never do anything. I can look without you. I doubt I'll find our dream house the first day."

CHAPTER TWO

T HE UCTI CAMPUS WAS A BUCOLIC REFUGE FROM THE surrounding streets of Westwood. Low-rise, Spanish Revival buildings sat among leafy trees and winding garden paths. Daniel parked his Mustang behind Brenda's police cruiser and followed his campus map to the Physics and Astronomy building. A patrolman stood guarding the front door, and directed him to the third floor. Daniel put on his shoe protectors and gloves, and opted for the stairs.

The third floor corridor was a silent series of closed doors, except for the office in which he found Brenda Jordan. He had been partnered with Brenda two years ago, when she was just a Sergeant, but she had rapidly climbed the ranks to Detective. Daniel liked working with her. She was smart, far more computer savvy than he, easy going and reliable. She was also looking unusually good lately. Her blond hair, once cut into an unflattering short style, had grown out to a shoulder-length bob. She had recently started working out regularly and had lost about twenty pounds, an improvement on her short, stocky body. Daniel hoped a new romantic relationship might account for the changes but Brenda was tightlipped about her personal life, and Daniel respected that.

Brenda was examining the body of a middle-aged man, slumped over his desk. The dregs of a cup of coffee had spilled on the desktop and carpet. The dead man had vomited onto his shirt. His face looked unusually flushed.

Daniel took in the scene. "Who was he?"

"His name is Edwin Larramore, Professor of Astronomy. One of his graduate students came in to work with him this morning and found him like this."

"Heart attack?" Daniel asked. "Stroke, perhaps?"

"Don't know," Brenda said. "I guess the autopsy will tell us, but I thought, just in case, we should have the crime scene team collect some vomit and coffee samples. It looks as if he made himself a cup with that fancy machine, drank most of it, threw up and died."

"You have a suspicious mind," Daniel said. "But, I agree."

"Suspicion is in my job description," Brenda said.

"Any history of heart disease?"

"The graduate student didn't think so, but we'll need to ask his wife. I have his wallet and cell phone. His address is on his driver's license."

Daniel examined the phone. There was a missed international call at 8:35 a.m. and a voicemail. He played it on speakerphone so that Brenda could hear.

"Dr. Larramore, this is Sven Pierrson from the Nobel Prize committee in Stockholm. I have not been able to reach you directly at any of your numbers, but I am calling to notify you that you have been awarded this year's Nobel Prize in Physics. Please return my call at your earliest opportunity."

"No shit," Brenda said. "We've got a dead Nobel Prize winner. Looks like he died before he knew."

"Where is the graduate student?" Daniel asked.

"Down the hall, in the student lounge. He's pretty shaken up. I figured you'd want to talk to him. His name is Kumar Aggarwal."

"Thanks. I'll do that while you wait for the lab team and the medical examiner," Daniel said.

Brenda nodded.

Daniel stripped his gloves and walked to the lounge. It was occupied by a tall, skinny Indian man in his early twenties, wearing a pair of neatly pressed jeans and a navy polo shirt. He was holding tight to a mug of tea and pacing the floor when Daniel arrived.

"Mr. Aggarwal, I'm Detective Ross," Daniel said. "Thank you for waiting. I just have a few questions for you, and then you can go home." Daniel thought Aggarwal looked ill. His face had a green tinge and his hands seemed to be trembling.

Aggarwal nodded. "What do you need to know?"

"What time did you come in this morning?"

Aggarwal stopped pacing and looked at his watch. "It was a little after nine o'clock. The professor asked me to meet him here, so we could begin the analysis of our new data."

"Do you normally work on Saturdays?"

"Frequently," Aggarwal said. "Sundays too. Professor Larramore expected his students to be available all the time, when new information needed to be processed."

"What kind of information?" Daniel asked.

"We're searching for Earth-like planets around other stars. Each time we observe, we obtain a huge amount of data and it takes a long time to go through it to find the subtle changes we are seeking. Dr. Larramore was dedicated to the search and expected his students to be productive."

"I see," Daniel said. "When you arrived this morning, what did you do?"

"I went directly to the Professor's office to let him know I'd arrived. I knocked and when there was no answer, I tried the door. When I opened it, I saw him lying over the desk. He looked ill."

"What did you do?"

"I went in and asked if he was all right, or needed help. When he didn't respond, I touched his wrist to see if I could feel a pulse. His body was cold and I realized he was dead, so I called 911."

"I'm sure this experience must be very difficult for you," Daniel said. "We're going to need to notify his family. Do you happen to know his wife?"

Aggarwal nodded. "She's on the faculty in the Chemistry department. Her name is Carolyn Larramore. You should probably notify Dr. George Taylor, our department chairman, as well. I'm sure he would want to break the news to the rest of the faculty and Dr. Larramore's students."

"Thank you," Daniel said. "Why don't you write down your contact information for me, in case I have any additional questions for you, and then you can leave."

Aggarwal shook his head. "I should probably get back to work. Dr. Larramore wouldn't have wanted me to go home."

When Daniel returned to Larramore's office, Dr. Bill Pincus, one of his favorite medical examiners, was bent over the body.

"Hi, Doc," Daniel said. "What do you think?"

"I think I need an autopsy and a toxicology screen,"

Pincus answered. "That should tell us if it was a natural death or suicide."

"Or murder?" Daniel asked.

"I'm not ruling out anything," Pincus said. "I'll let you know when we have the results."

Daniel motioned to Brenda to join him. Now came the worst part of any case, informing the family.

CHAPTER THREE

Daniel and Brenda sat in the Larramore's living room and watched as a tear trickled down Dr. Carolyn Larramore's face. It was a pretty face, wholesome and without makeup, dusted with light freckles, and surrounded by a short corona of curly, light brown hair. She looked like a college student, not like the faculty member she was. She was dressed in a pair of low-cut jeans and a tight-fitting workout shirt that outlined the bulge of her pregnant belly.

"It doesn't make sense," she said. "Edwin was in perfect health."

"Are you sure, Dr. Larramore?" Daniel asked. "No possible heart disease or high blood pressure?"

"Absolutely not. Edwin just had a complete physical. He was a health nut. He spent at least an hour a day working out. He even changed his diet to vegan."

"Had he been depressed lately?"

She shook her head. "Edwin had no reason to be depressed. He had made an astonishing discovery. Just this morning, I got a call from the Nobel Prize committee. He's been awarded the Physics Prize for this year. I wonder if he even knew?"

That statement resulted in more tears welling up and dripping down her face. She brushed them away with the back of her hand.

"What was his discovery?" Brenda asked.

"Astronomers have been seeking earth-sized planets with orbits in what is called the habitable, or Goldilocks Zone. That means the planet's distance from its sun results in a climate where it is possible for water to exist. Edwin was the first to demonstrate that one of these planets had an atmosphere with water and oxygen. Of the thousands of planets that have been discovered, this is the first one with the potential for life. He just published an article on it in Nature, the most prestigious of the scientific journals. He was riding high. Why would he have been depressed? You aren't suggesting that he committed suicide? That would be absurd."

"I'm afraid we won't know the cause of death until the autopsy is complete, Dr. Larramore," Daniel said. "We'll notify you when you can have his body for the funeral. We are so sorry for your loss."

Carolyn placed her hands on her bulging abdomen. "It's likely to be a very big funeral."

The tears continued to flow silently as she got up and showed them to the door.

"I hate this part of the job," Brenda said, as they headed back to the car. "She was remarkably composed though. I'm used to more sobbing and hysteria."

Daniel nodded. "Some people only break down in private. She's probably still in shock."

"Why do you suppose they call it the Goldilocks Zone? I don't get it," Brenda said.

Daniel grinned. "Didn't your mother ever read you *Goldilocks and the Three Bears*? Goldilocks explores the bears' cottage and finds three bowls of porridge. One is too hot. One is too cold, and one is just right. Come on, let's go talk to Dr. Taylor and then we can break for lunch."

George Taylor was Daniel's idea of the quintessential college professor. Tall and skinny, he was dressed in faded corduroy slacks and a plaid flannel shirt. A pair of gold, wire-rimmed glasses perched on his hawk-like nose, veiling his light blue eyes. Untidy white hair stood up around a large bald spot and he was sucking on a pipe stem. If only he had a mustache, he'd have resembled Albert Einstein.

"What is this about, Detective?" Taylor asked.

"Can we sit down?" Daniel asked. "I have some bad news to tell you."

Taylor's face blanched, but he said nothing. He waved Daniel and Brenda in the direction of the living room sofa.

Daniel cleared his throat. "One of your faculty, Dr. Edwin Larramore, was found dead this morning in his office, by one of his graduate students."

Taylor's jaw dropped, but Daniel noticed a flash of what almost seemed like relief on his face.

"That's terrible news," he said. "Forgive me, Detectives, but I thought for a minute that something might have happened to one of my children. How did Edwin die? Heart attack?"

"We don't know yet," Brenda said. "The coroner is taking the body for an autopsy. There should be an answer in a few days."

"We thought you should know," Daniel said. "Someone needs to break the news to his students and to the rest of your department. Were you aware, sir, that Dr. Larramore had just won a Nobel Prize?"

Taylor nodded. "Someone from the committee called me early this morning, looking for Edwin's contact numbers. What a tragedy, that he should die at the peak of his profession. Have you told his wife yet?"

"We just came from her home," Brenda said. "She's understandably very shaken."

"I'll ask my wife, Barbara, to go over there and see if we can help. Is there anything else Detectives?"

Daniel shook his head. "We are sorry. His death seems like a great loss for science."

Taylor nodded as he escorted them to the door.

"I guess that's all we need to do now, except for the paperwork," Daniel said to Brenda as they left.

Perhaps it wasn't too late for him to join Hannah for the remainder of her house hunt.

CHAPTER FOUR

THE REALTOR AND I WERE ON OUR FOURTH HOUSE when Daniel phoned. My head was beginning to spin. So far, the houses were either too old, too small or too garish. Jackie had done a valiant job of sticking to my criteria of location, price and number of bedrooms, but it wasn't easy. The real estate market was hot right now, and anything reasonably priced often went quickly with multiple offers. I was beginning to despair of ever finding anything suitable and feeling quite nostalgic for the little Craftsman bungalow in Pasadena where Ben and I had lived. House hunting with my late husband was quite a different experience from doing it on my own. Ben had been an architect and he had an ability, which I lacked, to separate the contents from the container. Ben could see the bones of a house and imagine what it would look like when he was done with it. I had trouble getting past people's bad taste in furniture or the bland sameness of homes that had been staged. My long marriage to Ben had, however, taught me to distinguish an architecturally interesting house from a cookie-cutter tract, and so far, I hadn't seen any.

"So, was it murder?" I asked.

"Too soon to tell, but I think not," Daniel answered. "Is it too late for me to join you?"

"I'd love it," I said. "How about lunch first? I need a break. CPK?"

"Meet you there in fifteen minutes," he said.

"Join us?" I said to Jackie.

She shook her head. "I'm going to stop in my office and check the listings to see if I missed anything. I'll call you if there's another house we should see today."

Sounded good to me. She probably wanted to give me a chance to discuss the prospects with Daniel.

By the time Daniel arrived, I had ordered his favorite barbecue chicken salad and a pepperoni pizza. He slid into the booth and helped himself to my iced tea with a sigh of relief.

"So, who died?" I asked.

"You'll probably read about it in tomorrow's paper, so no harm in discussing it," he said. "College professor named Edwin Larramore. The sad thing is that the guy had just been awarded the Nobel Prize in physics, but probably was dead when the committee called his cell phone."

"Sometimes life is just not fair," I said. "You sure it wasn't foul play?"

Daniel laughed. "Pretty sure, but I treated his office like a crime scene just to be certain. The hard part was breaking the news to his pregnant wife."

"Pregnant? Not Carolyn Larramore?"

"I'm afraid so. Is she your patient?"

I nodded. "I've taken care of her for several years. I really like her. How awful."

Daniel reached over and squeezed my hand. "If anyone knows how it feels to lose your husband during a pregnancy, you do. I'm relieved to know she has such a kind and empathic obstetrician."

I wondered if I should call her. Then I realized I wouldn't be able to explain how I'd found out. Better to wait until the death was reported in the papers. I would certainly go to the funeral, and try to be especially attentive during her next appointment. At least, it wasn't another homicide.

CHAPTER FIVE

IT WAS TUESDAY MORNING, AND DANIEL WAS JUST finishing his second cup of police station coffee when the phone rang. Brenda looked up from her computer at the adjoining desk.

Daniel picked up the phone. "Detective Ross speaking."

"It was homicide," said Bill Pincus.

"What?" Daniel said. "How? Who? Which corpse?"

"Dr. Larramore. We found high quantities of arsenic and nickel, in a consistent, four-to-one ratio, in the blood, stomach contents, coffee cup and the remaining ground espresso. Someone poisoned him."

"Poor bastard. Was it rat poison or an insecticide?" Daniel asked.

"We don't think so. There aren't any known insecticides or pesticides containing arsenic and nickel. The major ones, which are no longer legal to manufacture in the United States, contain sodium and calcium. That's not to say that supplies aren't still available of unused old product, but that wouldn't explain the nickel."

"So, what was it?"

"We don't know yet. We'll have to run a mass spectrometry and possibly some other spectroscopic analyses to pin it down. We're dealing with a murder at an institute where people are doing all kinds of scientific research. Who knows what weird compounds someone might be working on?" Bill said.

"So, you're telling me, I'm going to have to wait awhile to identify the murder weapon," Daniel said.

"I'm afraid so."

Daniel hung up the phone and turned to Brenda.

"I heard," she said. "Poison. What kind?"

"Some unusual arsenic compound. We need to start over."

"Who would want to murder a Nobel Prize winner?" Brenda asked.

"The usual suspects, I imagine: jealous academic competitors, disenfranchised students, betrayed wives, angry mistresses, people who owed him money, or visa versa. It needs to be someone with access to his office and his coffee supply. We're going to need to learn a good deal more about this man."

"So, where do you want to start, boss?" Brenda asked.

"We should probably talk to the head of campus security. But first, we need to break the news to his wife," Daniel said.

CHAPTER SIX

MY DAY IN THE OFFICE BEGAN WITH CAROLYN Larramore's twenty-four week pregnancy check-up. She was thirty-two years old and hadn't required any invasive genetic testing, but she had recently completed a routine structural scan, and a test for alpha-fetal protein levels, to be certain there was no spina bifida or other congenital anomalies. All had appeared normal.

When I entered the exam room, she was sitting quietly on the table, her face set in a serious expression, without its usual smile.

"Carolyn," I said. "I saw the newspaper yesterday. I'm so sorry about your husband."

I'd expected she might break into tears, or need a hug. I'd supplied any number of those to patients in crisis, but she just looked at me.

"I hadn't planned on being a single mother, Dr. Kline," she said. "I don't know how."

I don't usually share my personal life with patients, but this situation seemed to call for it.

"I can help if you'd like to talk about it," I said. "I lost my husband when I was pregnant as well. So far, I've survived six years of single parenthood, and I can tell you one thing for sure. Having a child to look after will make the loss a little easier to bear."

"I feel so guilty," she said. This time the tears began to flow.

"Guilty about what?" I asked, laying a hand gently on her shoulder.

"I was going to leave him. Edwin was so difficult, so completely self-centered. I was miserable in our marriage. I'd made up my mind to ask for a divorce, when I discovered I was pregnant, and then I couldn't leave. Everyone thinks I'm a devastated, bereaved wife, but all I feel is a sense of relief. Please don't repeat this to anyone."

"Of course, I won't," I said. "But don't feel guilty. Nothing you did or felt could have prevented his death."

"I should never have married him. I was a graduate student. He was a brilliant professor. I was mesmerized and flattered that he was interested in me."

"Were you in his classes?" I asked.

"Just one. I've always been interested in astronomy, so I took his introductory class for fun. All my other classes were in the chemistry department. To Edwin's credit, he didn't ask me out until after I was no longer his student."

"When did you get married?"

"When I graduated. I finished my PhD in Chemistry and was offered an assistant professorship at NYU. I turned it down to marry him. But the only position I could get here was a non-tenured adjunct slot, running the freshman chemistry labs. I think they save it for wives of high profile faculty. Anyway, my career is at a standstill, I'm pregnant, and I'm at a loss as to what to do next."

"Try taking it one day at a time," I said. "Will you be all right financially?"

"I think so, at least for awhile," she said. "The house is community property. At least I won't have to move out. I don't think I could handle that right now. Eventually, I may have to."

"What about the funeral? Is there one scheduled?"

She nodded. "The department chair took over the arrangements for me. They're releasing Edwin's body tomorrow. There's going to be a university-wide memorial for him on Friday afternoon. It will probably be huge. I don't even own a black suit that fits over my belly."

"Maybe that should be your project for today," I said. "Can you lie down?"

Carolyn leaned back. I measured her uterus and listened with the doptone to the fetal heart rate, entering the data into her chart. Everything looked normal.

"Baby seems fine," I said. "I should see you in four weeks for your next appointment, and then we'll go to every other week. If I can help in any way, if you'd like to come in and talk after office hours, please call me. I really am here for you. I know from experience that venting to a sympathetic ear can sometimes make you feel better."

She smiled at me. "It already has, Dr. Kline."

CHAPTER SEVEN

WHEN DANIEL PHONED CAROLYN LARRAMORE FROM his car, she wasn't at home or in her office. He decided not to leave a message. Instead, he drove to the University, to meet with the head of campus security.

He had previously met Steve Kowalski when the body was found, and his impression was of a seasoned professional. Kowalski was a big man with a Slavic face, a gray mustache, and a large paunch. He had a small office with old, wooden university furniture, and comfortable chairs with worn leather upholstery.

He greeted Daniel and Brenda with a smile and motioned for them to sit down. The smile turned to astonishment when Daniel broke the news.

"Homicide? You've got to be kidding," he said.

"I wish we were," Daniel said. "The autopsy proves the death wasn't natural. I can't release any of the details, but I need your help. What are the security arrangements for the Physics and Astronomy building? Who would have access to Larramore's office? Are there cameras and video feed?"

Kowalski shrugged. "It isn't a high security building. It

was built in the 1930's, like much of the campus. There are security cameras at the back and front entrance, and in the basement, because the labs with the expensive equipment are there, but none on the floors where the faculty have offices."

"Who has access to the building?" Brenda asked.

"During the day, the doors are unlocked and anyone can come in. After 10 p.m., security locks the doors and there's a card keypad for access. All the faculty and graduate students have pass cards."

"What about the faculty offices?" Daniel asked.

"Medeco keys. They're only issued to the faculty member. The housekeeping staff, and the department chair, have passkeys to all the offices."

"Do the professors normally keep their offices locked when they're not there?" Daniel asked.

"Depends," Kowalski said. "If they're in the building for the day, teaching, grabbing lunch, taking a leak, they might not always lock their door."

"So, if someone wanted to murder Larramore," Brenda said, "they could enter the building at any time, enter Larramore's office if it was unlocked, or somehow obtain a passkey."

Kowalski nodded.

"We'll need the video feeds and the keypad data starting Thursday night through Saturday," Daniel said.

"I'll have someone pull them and send them over to the station," Kowalski said.

"Thanks. Keep this quiet for now. I haven't told his wife yet. I'm going to call her again in a few minutes."

As they walked to their car, Daniel tried Carolyn again. There was still no answer and her cell phone went to voicemail.

"I wonder where she is," Brenda said.

Daniel shrugged. "We need to find out the last time Larramore was seen having coffee in his office. If he drank coffee without a problem Friday, then the killer must have added the poison later that day, or Saturday morning, before Larramore got to the office."

"How about, while we're waiting for Carolyn to get home, we find ourselves some graduate students?" Brenda suggested.

Kumar Aggarwal answered his cell phone promptly and agreed to meet Daniel and Brenda in his office in the Physics building. The student offices were the size of a linen closet, but contained a desk, bookcase, computer terminal, and an extra chair.

Daniel motioned to Brenda to sit, and perched himself on the edge of a small file cabinet.

"Some questions have arisen about Dr. Larramore's death, and I have some additional things to ask you," he said.

Aggarwal nodded, tapping a pencil nervously on his desktop. "I'm happy to answer, but I don't know what you're looking for."

"Tell me about the members of your research group. Who are they? What are they working on, and how far along are they in their research?"

Aggarwal relaxed, a puzzled expression on his face.

"Dr. Larramore had three graduate students. I've been with him for four years and am in the middle of writing my thesis. Tomas Rivera is a year behind me. Suzanne Baron is a first year graduate student. She just started in our group. I don't know if she's chosen a thesis topic yet, but she'll definitely have to choose a new advisor."

"What about yourself and Mr. Rivera?"

"I spoke to one of the other members of my thesis committee. He's willing to supervise the remainder of my work, as I am almost done writing and have already published two papers," Aggarwal said. "I don't know what Tomas is doing yet, or how far along he is with his research. I can tell you he hasn't published anything and he's been struggling with his data analysis."

"Did Mr. Rivera have a problem with Dr. Larramore?" Daniel asked.

"More like Dr. Larramore had a problem with Tomas. Dr. Larramore made no secret of his displeasure with Tomas's lack of progress. What Dr. Larramore didn't know was that Tomas has been waiting tables on weekends to help his family out financially. They have very little money. But his job has definitely interfered with his ability to work on his research."

"Why didn't Tomas tell Larramore?" Brenda asked.

"I imagine he was afraid of being kicked out of the group. Extra jobs aren't against the rules, but they're not encouraged. Our graduate stipends aren't very generous, but Dr. Larramore wasn't the kind of man who would be sympathetic to Tomas's situation."

Daniel nodded. "I see. Tell me more about yourself. You said you'd already published?"

"We published two papers in Nature a few months ago," Aggarwal said, nodding. "We identified a rocky planet, about twice the size of earth, around a nearby class K star. We were able to demonstrate that it had an atmosphere containing oxygen and water. It's a remarkable discovery, the first of its kind."

"And you were involved with Dr. Larramore in making that discovery?" Daniel asked.

Aggarwal reached into his desk and pulled out two

volumes of a scientific journal. He opened each to a page marked with a yellow post-it and handed them to Daniel.

"I actually analyzed the spectroscopy that identified the water and oxygen," he said.

Daniel looked at the papers. The authors were Larramore, E. and Aggarwal, K. The first paper reported the presence of a signal identifying water. The second paper, in the following volume, demonstrated the presence of oxygen.

"Was this the discovery for which Dr. Larramore was awarded the Nobel Prize?" he asked.

Aggarwal nodded. "That, and his contribution to developing the transit method for detecting extrasolar planets."

"What does that mean?" Daniel asked.

"When an extrasolar planet passes between its star and the earth, the amount of light we see from that star decreases. The extent of the decrease, and the amount of time that we see less light, can be used to calculate the size of the planet and its distance from its sun. Prior to the development of the transit method, all we could find were giant planets, the size of Jupiter."

"It sounds as if that discovery alone might have earned him the Prize," Brenda said.

"He wasn't the only one," Aggarwal said. "Another group published the method simultaneously. I suspect it was our more recent discovery and publications that tipped the balance in his favor for the Prize."

"Impressive," Daniel said.

"Does this mean you found a planet that might contain life? Or one that we humans could colonize if we ruin this one?" Brenda asked.

Aggarwal laughed. "Even if it is, I'm afraid it's out of our reach. It's eighty light years away. In galactic terms, just around the corner, but with our current technology, it would probably take about eight hundred thousand years to send a probe there, and another eighty years for the probe to transmit its data back. By that time, there may not even be any humans left on earth."

"That's a depressing thought," Daniel said. "No chance of warp drive?"

"I'm afraid not," Aggarwal said. "That only happens on Star Trek."

"Is there anyone else in the group?" Brenda asked.

"We have a visiting Professor from Australia. His name is Oliver Wilson. He's been here about nine months."

"Would you say Dr. Larramore was an accessible advisor?" Daniel asked. "Were you students constantly in and out of his office, conferring with him?"

"Not really," Aggarwal said. "He had specific office hours when he would meet with us. Otherwise, he didn't like to be disturbed."

"You mentioned, when we spoke to you on Saturday morning, that his door was unlocked when you came in. Does he usually leave it unlocked when he's in?" Brenda asked.

"Why wouldn't he? Faculty only lock their doors when they leave for the day. Most of them don't bother if they're in the building. Students always knock before trying a door. Sometimes an office is empty and we just come back later."

"I noticed that Dr. Larramore had a very fancy coffee machine in his office. Did your research group often get together for coffee?" Daniel asked.

"Definitely not. Dr. Larramore was very possessive of his espresso and didn't share. We got the cheap stuff in the student lounge. Why are you asking?"

"Just trying to get a picture of how he related to his

students," Brenda said. "Did you, by any chance, notice him having coffee on Friday?"

"He started every morning with a latte. It was a ritual with him. Is there something funny about his death?" Aggarwal asked.

"We don't have the autopsy report yet," Daniel said. This was stretching the truth a bit, but it was true. The medical examiner hadn't identified the substance that had killed Larramore. Besides, he wasn't going to reveal anything to a student, until he had informed Larramore's wife that it was a homicide.

"We're just doing some preliminary homework. Thank you for your cooperation," Daniel said.

"So," Brenda said, as they walked down the hall, "if we assume he had his latte as usual, we're looking for someone who entered the office when he wasn't there, sometime on Friday or early Saturday morning. I wonder how many people go in and out of that building in twenty-four hours."

It was very late in the afternoon before Carolyn Larramore finally answered Daniel's call and agreed to see them.

She answered the door looking wan and tired.

"We're sorry to disturb you, Dr. Larramore," Daniel said. "I tried to reach you earlier, but you weren't answering any of your phones."

"I was at my obstetrician's in the morning," Carolyn replied. "And then I had to shop for a black maternity outfit for the funeral. I always turn my cell phone off when I'm at the doctor's office. I guess I forgot to turn it back on."

"No problem," Daniel said. So, she'd been at Hannah's office. He wondered what Hannah's assessment of Carolyn might be. Not that she would share it. She was very protective of her patients.

"We wouldn't be here if it wasn't important. Can we come in?"

Carolyn nodded and motioned them into the den, where they sat on comfortable wing chairs while she stretched out on the sofa.

"What is it?" she asked.

"Dr. Larramore, the medical examiner notified us this morning that your husband's death wasn't natural. We're classifying it a homicide."

"What?" She looked at them with a stunned expression.

"I'm afraid it's true," Brenda said. "We can't release the autopsy details yet, but we're hoping you can help us find out who murdered him. Did your husband have any enemies that you know of? Was there anyone who hated him enough to kill him, a student, perhaps, or a colleague?"

Carolyn bent her head and covered her face with her hands. She took several deep breaths, as if she were practicing Lamaze. Then she looked up.

"Edwin wasn't the kindest or most considerate person. He worked his students very hard and was very demanding, but they all managed to do good research and get good jobs because of the prestige of working with him. I can't imagine any one of them would hate him enough to kill him."

"What about his friends? Who were they?" Daniel asked.

"Edwin didn't have friends. He had colleagues and we didn't socialize with any of them. Our social life, the little there was, revolved around my friends."

"Did he get along with his colleagues?" Daniel asked.

Carolyn shrugged. "I'm not aware of any enmity. They were all working in different areas of astronomy, so there wasn't any competition, and Edwin didn't collaborate with anyone in his department."

"Who were his competitors?" Brenda asked.

"There are two other large groups that work in the area of discovering extrasolar planets. One is at Berkeley, run by Professor Lee Wang. Lee was at MIT with Edwin during graduate school. The other group is in New York, at Columbia. Professor Isobel Martin runs that group. The competition between the three groups is pretty intense."

"Are there any competitors working in Los Angeles?" Daniel asked. "I don't imagine that Doctors Wang and Martin were here this weekend."

"Oh, but Dr. Isobel Martin was, Detective." Carolyn said. "The Institute has been sponsoring a symposium on extra-solar planet research. It began on Friday. Edwin gave the keynote address Friday morning. And Dr. Martin is Edwin's ex-wife."

"The plot thickens," Brenda said as she slid into the passenger seat of Daniel's car. "I know she's pointing us at the ex. But I can't shake the thought that Carolyn Larramore is a chemist. And she would certainly have unlimited access to her husband's coffee."

"Of course. The spouse is always number one on the suspect list, " Daniel said. "I didn't want to ask her about her research or access to chemicals just yet. I think we can find out those things without putting her on the defensive. Let's head back to the station and look at the Institute website. We need to do some background research on all those people, get some photos, and try to identify everyone who entered the building during the key timeframe. Tomorrow, we can go through all those hours of video."

CHAPTER EIGHT

W HEN I GOT HOME FROM THE OFFICE, I FOUND ZOE IN the kitchen busily working on her first grade homework. Emilia, our housekeeper, was putting the final touches on beef lasagna and tossing a salad.

"Smells yummy," I said.

"Zoe helped," Emilia said. "I teach her to be a good cook."

"You're a hard act to follow," I said.

Over the past five years, Emilia and I had worked our way through my favorite cookbook. I picked the recipes and stocked the ingredients, and she turned them into magic. I was glad she was teaching Zoe. My mother never taught me to cook.

"Can you check my addition, Mommy?" Zoe asked.

I deposited my purse on the kitchen counter and placed a kiss on her forehead.

"Let's see," I said.

Zoe handed me her sheet of math problems.

"It's perfect," I said. "I can't find a single mistake."

"I'm good at numbers," she said.

"Any other homework for today?" I asked.

She made a face and handed me several sheets of paper that appeared to be testing her knowledge of vowel sounds.

"This is so boring," she said. "The teacher is teaching the class to read, but I can already do that. She gave us these silly books that are much too easy."

"Would you like me to talk to your teacher?" I asked. "Maybe I can get her to give you something more interesting to read."

Zoe gave me one of her enchanting smiles. I took that as a yes.

I went upstairs, changed out of my office clothes, and called Daniel's cell.

"Hi sweetie. Just wondering if you're going to make it home for dinner?"

"I am," he said. "I should be there in about an hour. It's been an interesting day."

"Can't wait to hear about it," I said.

Daniel's interesting day was rarely, if ever, dinner table conversation in front of Zoe. We tried to keep it simple. Daniel's job was catching bad guys and his boss didn't allow him to talk about the details. Zoe was more interested in discussing the latest developments in school.

I didn't hear about Edwin Larramore's murder until Zoe was in the den reading, and Daniel and I were doing the dishes.

"We're trying to keep the case details quiet but it won't be long before the media learns that he was poisoned," Daniel said.

"With what?" I asked.

"Not sure. It was some exotic arsenic compound. The killer put it in a bag of ground espresso in Larramore's office. He died when he had his morning latte. The lab is still trying to figure out exactly what the chemical was. Poison and arsenic are details we aren't releasing yet," he said.

"My lips are sealed. Any suspects?"

"The usual. His wife, his students, his academic competitors. It's going to be a complicated investigation. I know you saw Carolyn Larramore this morning. Is there anything you can tell me?"

I shook my head. Daniel would probably be interested in knowing how unhappily married the Larramores were, but I couldn't tell him. Patient confidentiality was sacred. It was also illegal for me to reveal anything about a patient to anyone not directly involved in her medical care. No matter. I couldn't visualize Carolyn as a murder suspect.

"She told me there was going to be a memorial service on Friday at the Institute. I thought I'd go and pay my respects."

"Good idea," Daniel said. "I think Brenda and I should go as well."

"We probably shouldn't be seen together," I said. "I don't think Carolyn should know that I'm engaged to the investigating detective."

CHAPTER NINE

T HE INVESTIGATING DETECTIVE AND HIS PARTNER spent a tedious Wednesday putting together data from the Institute website and the security videos. Brenda had confiscated a large corkboard and was busy pinning on photos and bios of potential suspects and witnesses. She had worked her way through all of the astronomy faculty, Larramore's graduate group, and the speakers at the UCTI symposium. She pinned all the photos to the board so they could identify them from the videos.

"We probably need to interview all the astronomy faculty, but as far as I can tell, Carolyn was correct when she said no one else was working on extrasolar planets," Brenda said. "We've got black holes in the center of galaxies, super novas and microwave background radiation, but no planets."

"What's microwave background?" Daniel asked.

"Stuff left over from the big bang," she said. "But it doesn't sound like anything Larramore was working on."

Daniel was working his way through the chemistry department, looking for people whose research might involve arsenic compounds. Carolyn was apparently a biochemist. She had obtained her PhD at the Institute. Her current research involved working out the chemical pathways for tumor suppressor genes PTEN and P53. Daniel had no idea what that meant but thought that cancer research was unlikely to involve arsenic. But that didn't mean that she didn't have access to it. He realized he didn't know anywhere near enough chemistry to make any judgments and decided to fax the list of research projects to Bill Pincus, to see if he thought any of them were worth further investigation.

The Extrasolar Planet Symposium had started on Friday, and gone through Sunday morning. They looked at the program, checked on the bios of all the speakers, and obtained photos to crosscheck with the videos. Brenda had paid special attention to Isobel Martin.

Daniel looked at the information carefully. Over the past ten years, Isobel and her group at Columbia had discovered over five hundred extrasolar planets, and had published more than a hundred papers in prestigious journals. She received her PhD from MIT the same year as Edwin Larramore, so they must have been graduate students together.

Daniel reminded himself to check on her marriage and divorce dates. She would need to be interviewed, but Daniel suspected that she had probably left town after the conference. He would need to call her, unless she came back to Los Angeles for the memorial.

There was little information about the students, other than a photograph and a notation about their undergraduate degree. Brenda printed the photos for the board. They assigned one of the murder team to check and see if anyone had a past police record, and to see if any additional information could be extracted from Facebook.

"Who ever imagined that we'd be using Facebook to crack cases?" Brenda asked.

"Current and cold," Daniel said. "I'm still not going to join it. The privacy issues give me the creeps. It might even be dangerous for anyone working in law enforcement to be on it. Who wants criminals to be able to access your personal information?"

"I keep my page totally private," Brenda said. "I don't really post much on it, or use it for anything other than access when I'm on a case."

"I'd keep it that way, if I were you," Daniel said. "Cops are walking targets."

By lunchtime, they were ready to tackle the videos. Daniel tracked Larramore's movements, and Brenda kept an eye open for Carolyn.

Larramore had come into the building at 8:30 a.m. on Friday, left at 9:45 a.m., presumably for the symposium, and returned at 4:15 p.m..

"Do you suppose he left his office unlocked all that time?" Brenda asked.

"Seems unlikely," Daniel said. "Did you see any sign of Carolyn entering the building?"

Brenda shook her head.

"Could she have put the poison in the espresso at home, and just given it to him to take to the office?"

"I don't think so," Brenda said. "There was very little coffee left. He was obviously running out and needed a new supply. If he'd brought a big bag of poisoned coffee from home, he'd have been dead a lot sooner. I think someone added the arsenic to the little that was left in the bottom of the bag."

"She's still high on my list," Daniel said. "She's a chemist with probable access to arsenic. And she may have a spare key to the office."

"Let's see who else we can identify."

The security videos were frustrating. Large numbers of undergraduate students came and went for classes. Graduate students and faculty also accessed the building during work hours. Actual faces were hard to come by, obscured by hoodies or baseball caps, or simply by people facing away from the camera as they came up the stairs. It was clear that there was no hope of identifying everyone who had entered the building that day. At best, they could scan the videos for the people who interested them most and hope for the best.

By five o'clock, Daniel had a headache and Brenda suggested they quit for the day.

"Good idea," Daniel said. "You go on home. I'm going to make up an interview list and distribute it in the morning. There are too many for the two of us."

Brenda shut down her computer, grabbed her purse and headed out the door.

Daniel decided to send the video, along with the relevant photos, to the video lab, to see if someone with more expertise could enhance it.

Then, he made his list and called Hannah to let her know he was on his way home.

CHAPTER TEN

I GOT HOME EARLY ON WEDNESDAY, AS USUAL. I DON'T see patients on Wednesday afternoons. Instead, I use the time for paperwork, bill paying and running errands. Wednesday was also Skype day with my parents on the East Coast. They were besotted with their grandchild, and we never allowed a week to elapse without a call from Zoe.

My parents, Esther and Max Kramer, had moved from Brooklyn to Miami a few years ago, when my dad finally sold his export business and retired. By that time, a majority of their friends and neighbors had gotten tired of the New York winters, and had migrated south. I had been skeptical. My parents had always been invetcrate New Yorkers. They went to the theatre regularly, had a subscription to the New York Philharmonic at Lincoln Center, and were members of the Metropolitan Museum of Art. I was afraid they would find Miami a cultural wasteland. Somehow, they adjusted. I supposed that having friends to spend time with was ultimately more important than having concert tickets. I tried to make it out to Miami at least once a year with Zoe, preferably in the winter, but this year, I wanted them to meet Daniel, so I encouraged them to come to Los Angeles.

Until I was certain about my relationship with Daniel, I hadn't mentioned him to my parents. It had been so long since I'd dated, I was afraid my mother would start making wedding plans, before I had a clue as to whether the relationship would work.

I had told my mother about him, when he moved in, and had just broken the news of our engagement. My folks were flying in for the Thanksgiving weekend. The prospect of their meeting Daniel made me more than a little nervous. My mother rarely censored her curiosity and was apt to ask rather nosy questions. She would have done well as a detective, interviewing suspects. I'd made hotel reservations for them, at a small, art deco hotel on Ocean Avenue in Santa Monica, so that they could walk to the Promenade. Mom loved to shop.

Zoe and I usually called at about 5:00 p.m., allowing for the three-hour time difference. My parents looked great. Dad had a tan (despite my warnings about sunscreen and hats) and had lost some weight. His gray hair and neatly trimmed mustache always made me think of a much older version of Clark Gable. Mom had adopted tropical sundresses in bright colors. I had inherited my red hair and light skin from her. Unlike my father, she dressed like a dermatologist when she went outdoors, with long sleeves and a big floppy hat. She had always dressed fashionably, not a skill set I had inherited. Both of them looked relaxed and happy.

"Zoe, darling, how's school?" Mom asked.

"It's good, Grandma. I can read better than anyone in my class."

"Of course, you can. Hannah, where's Daniel?" Daniel

had chatted with them on Skype a few times, but she was clearly anxious for a longer and more personal conversation.

"Working, Mom. He has a new case and it's complicated," I said.

"What kind of a new case?"

Mom had the habit of asking, even though I always gave her the same answer.

"You know Daniel isn't allowed to talk about his cases, even to me," I said.

She rolled her eyes to let me know how little she believed me and moved on to another topic. "Any luck with the house hunting?"

"Not so far, but we've only looked one weekend," I said.

"In my day, first a couple got married, then they got pregnant, and then they bought a house. Nowadays, everything is backwards."

"We thought we'd buy a house first. The prices aren't going to get any lower," I said. I wasn't going to touch the pregnant remark with a ten-foot pole.

"That's my girl," Dad commented. Thrift was a family virtue next to cleanliness and Godliness.

We went on to discuss the latest gossip about the Brooklyn friends in my parents' social circle, and Zoe said goodbye with an air-kiss. I gave my parents their hotel information and promised I'd be there to pick them up at the airport.

Daniel arrived home a few minutes later and gave both of us a big hug. He looked unusually tired. I followed him up to the bedroom where he changed into sweats and t-shirt.

"Long day?"

He nodded. "Just computer work, trying to obtain background material on all the people I need to interview. The security tapes weren't all that helpful. Hundreds of under-graduates go in and out every day. I'm hoping forensics will help us narrow down the possible suspects. Tomorrow, Brenda and I are interviewing the rest of Larramore's research group. Perhaps we'll come up with a few viable suspects."

CHAPTER ELEVEN

Tomas Rivera, Larramore's graduate student, looked exhausted. His eyes were bloodshot, with dark circles, and he had the sort of five-o'clock shadow which looked sexy on male models, but just made him look unkempt. His shirt was wrinkled, as though he'd slept in it, and his straight, dark hair was unruly. He opened the door of his office to Daniel's knock, rubbing his eyes as if he'd just gotten out of bed.

"Mr. Rivera, I'm Detective Ross and this is Detective Jordan. We just need a few minutes of your time."

Brenda took out a notebook and deposited herself opposite Thomas's chair, in the only extra seat. Tomas returned to his chair and Daniel perched himself on the corner of the desk.

"There will be a press conference this morning, announcing that the Coroner's office has ruled Dr. Larramore's death a homicide, Mr. Rivera. The news will be public very soon and we are now interviewing all the faculty and students."

Tomas's eyes opened wide. "How was he killed?" he asked.

"I'm afraid that is still confidential," Daniel said. "Can you tell me when was the last time you saw Dr. Larramore?"

"It was Friday morning," Tomas said. "All of our group went to the Extrasolar Planet Symposium to hear him make the keynote address."

"Did you return to the Astronomy building after his talk?"

"No. We had all been told to go to the Friday lectures. None of us worked that day."

"None of you stopped by your offices at lunchtime, or after the talks were over?"

"I don't know about anyone else, but I didn't. I had lunch at the symposium and went to my mother's house for dinner immediately after it was over," Tomas said.

"Is there someone who can confirm your presence at the conference?" Brenda asked.

"I was sitting next to Suzanne Baron. She's one of the other graduate students. I was with her until it was over."

"What about Saturday morning?" Daniel asked. "Did you come into work?"

"No, sir. I spent the day with my family. I didn't find out about Dr. Larramore until the next day, when Kumar called me."

"Tell me about your relationship with your advisor, Mr. Rivas. Did you like him? Did you get along? Was he satisfied with your work?" Daniel asked

Tomas hesitated. "Dr. Larramore was a very demanding advisor. He believed that nothing in a student's life should be as important as the research. I think he would have liked me to progress faster, but we certainly had a cordial relationship."

"What kind of work were you doing with him?" Brenda asked.

"I was looking at stars which are known to have planets, and measuring the amount of heavy elements, like iron, for example, that they contain. We were trying to see if there was any correlation between the amount of heavy elements and the presence of small, rocky, Earth-like planets."

"I see," Brenda said. "Did you find a relationship?"

"Not yet," Tomas said. "I don't have enough data."

"Mr. Rivas," Daniel said, "can you think of any reason anyone would want to kill your thesis advisor? Do you know anyone who hated him? Anyone who may have argued with him recently?"

Tomas ran a hand through his hair. His hesitation was palpable.

"Not really," Tomas finally said. "He was a well-respected scientist. I can't imagine why anyone would want to kill him."

"Well that wasn't useful," Brenda said as they walked down the hall. "I wonder what he really thinks about Larramore. Who's next on your list?"

"Let's go see Suzanne Baron," Daniel said. "I'd like to finish interviewing her and Oliver Wilson today. Her office is just down the hall."

As they continued to walk, Daniel felt his cell phone vibrating.

"Detective Ross," he said, answering the call.

"Daniel, Bill Pincus. I've got follow-up info for you."

Daniel motioned to Brenda to wait. "Great. What did you find out?"

"Here's the update on the forensics. There were lots of fingerprints all over the office. We need to send someone to take prints of all the graduate students and possibly the faculty for elimination purposes. We also need to print his wife. Unfortunately, the only prints on the mug and coffee machine were Larramore's, but there was one on the coffee bag. We also found a long blonde hair on the sofa in the office, that clearly wasn't his. Is Mrs. Larramore blonde?"

"Brown," Daniel said. "And not long."

Pincus continued. "I had one of the chemists review all the Chemistry department's research projects. He said none of them, as far as he could tell, would be using arsenic for anything. That's the bad news. The good news is that we did multiple spectroscopic analyses and have actually identified the compound. It's called Nickel Diarsine."

"What's it for?" Daniel asked.

"It's not for anything practical. We searched all the chemistry databases and found only two articles, published in the 1970's, in the Journal of the American Chemical Society. The work was done at UC San Diego. I emailed you the two reference papers and all the forensic information. Maybe you can track down the two guys who published the paper, if they're still alive."

"Where would someone get hold of, or make, a compound like this?" Daniel asked.

"It's certainly not available for sale in its present form. Theoretically, it could be synthesized. As I said, you need to track down the folks who published that paper. They might be able to tell you."

"Thanks, Bill," Daniel said. "Much appreciated."

He returned his cell to its case and quickly brought Brenda up to speed.

"Why don't you look at the names on the paper and have

someone at the station start tracking them while we finish our interviews?" she suggested.

"This is why I keep you around," Daniel said. "I only have half a brain when you aren't here."

Brenda grinned. Daniel retrieved his cell and went to his email. Then he called the station. When he was done, they proceeded to Suzanne Baron's office.

When they arrived, Suzanne was sitting at her computer, ostensibly at work, but it was obvious she was anxious. Her face looked puffy, as if she had been crying and there were traces of black mascara on her cheeks. The first thing Daniel noticed was that she was very attractive and had long, blonde hair. She wore a turquoise turtleneck sweater that accented her blue eyes, and her hands were beautifully manicured.

The two detectives seated themselves and Brenda took out her notebook.

"Thank you for meeting with us," Daniel said, after the introductions had been made.

"Is it true?" Suzanne asked. "Was he really murdered?"

"I'm afraid so," Daniel said. "That's why we're here. We need to establish the whereabouts of everyone associated with Dr. Larramore on Friday and on Saturday morning. Can you tell us where you were?"

"I was at the conference on Friday, with the rest of my research group."

"Did you stop in your office, prior to the conference?" Daniel asked.

Suzanne shook her head. "I went directly to the conference from home and was there all day."

"Who were you sitting with?" Brenda asked.

"I was with Tomas Rivera. Kumar and Oliver were in the row behind us."

"And were all of you there all day?" Daniel asked.

"Tomas and I were. We went to the luncheon together. I didn't see Kumar and Oliver at lunch, but it was a big room and they were probably at another table. We all left together at the end of the conference. Then I went home."

"Do you live with a roommate?" Brenda asked.

Suzanne nodded.

"What time did you get home and was your roommate there?" Daniel asked.

"I think I got back about 4:30. I live in an apartment just off campus. Melody, my roommate, came home shortly after I arrived."

Daniel nodded. "Tell me about Dr. Larramore. How well did you know him? What did you think of him as an advisor?"

"I'm a first year graduate student, so I'm mostly taking courses right now, but I knew from the moment I got here that I wanted to work with him. He was wonderful. Brilliant, charming, kind. I met with him several times to discuss possible thesis topics. I was going to choose one and start working on it next semester. I can't believe he's gone." A tear trickled down her face.

"Did you find him accessible?" Brenda asked. "Was he the kind of man who was available to his students?"

"Oh, yes," Suzanne breathed. "He was always willing to make time for me."

"Can you tell us where you were on Saturday morning?" Daniel asked.

"I was home," she said. "Melody and I went out for

breakfast around nine o'clock. Then I went back to the apartment to finish some class assignments."

"We'll need Melody's contact information," Brenda said. "Is there anything else you can tell us? Do you have any idea of who might have wanted to kill Dr. Larramore?"

The delicate white hands moved to hide her face as she shook her head. Tears trickled down her cheeks. "I can't begin to imagine."

"Well," said Brenda, as they left Suzanne's office. "That's a serious case of hero worship, if I've ever seen one. Her take on Larramore is obviously completely different from anyone else's, including his wife. I think the tears were genuine."

"I wonder if that blonde hair belonged to Suzanne. Do you think they were doing something more than discussing thesis topics on that sofa?" Daniel asked.

"My thought, precisely. We'd better have someone check on her alibi, but I'm betting it holds up," Brenda said. "Shall we talk to Oliver Wilson and then quit for the day?"

Daniel nodded.

Oliver Wilson was clearly not a graduate student. Daniel estimated his age at about forty. He was tall and trim, with a shock of straight blonde hair beginning to gray at his sideburns. His skin was tanned with wrinkles around hazel eyes and a strong nose and jaw. He wore a white shirt, crisply ironed, with rolled-up sleeves and open at the neck, along with faded jeans and a thick leather belt with a silver buckle. He exuded a sense of confidence and masculine self-assurance. He rose from his desk as Daniel and Brenda entered, and greeted them both with a handshake.

"Thank you for seeing us Dr. Wilson," Daniel said. "We just have a few questions."

"No problem," Wilson said. "Please, be seated." He waved them over to a small sofa and deposited himself in a comfortable armchair opposite it. The size of his office alone would have told Daniel that his status was professorial. Wilson leaned back in a relaxed posture, crossing his legs.

"How can I help you?" he asked. The accent was strongly Australian.

"What was your relationship to Dr. Edwin Larramore?" Daniel asked.

"We do similar research. I'm a professor at the Australian National University. This is my sabbatical year. I took advantage of it to come to Los Angeles as a visiting faculty member, and to collaborate with Larramore's group."

"How long have you been here?" Brenda asked.

"About nine months. My sabbatical will be over in January. That's summer in Australia."

"And what kind of collaboration were you involved in?" Daniel asked.

"Do you know anything about stars, Detective?" Wilson asked.

"Not much," Daniel said.

"Well, our sun is what is called a main sequence star. It's middle-sized and middle-aged and yellow. Much of the effort to find extrasolar Earth-like planets has focused on stars like our sun. However, the most common type of star in our galaxy is the type K star. They are smaller, redder and much older."

"And this is important because?" Daniel asked.

"Because they're not as hot, they live longer. Both Edwin Larramore and I have felt that these smaller stars might be good candidates for Earth-like planets. There is a great deal of data from the Kepler telescope that has yet to be analyzed, and we were both working on it, to see if we could identify some likely candidates. You probably know that the planet that had oxygen and water in its atmosphere was orbiting a class K star. Unfortunately, I wasn't the one who found that particular planet."

"Larramore discovered it?" Brenda asked.

"Actually, it was Kumar. Very smart guy. Very hard working."

"I'm a little confused," Brenda said. "If Kumar discovered the planet, and found the oxygen and water, how come Larramore was awarded the Nobel?"

Wilson laughed and shook his head. "Academia, Detective. The peons do the work and the big boss gets the lion's share of the credit. That's how it's always been."

"Hardly seems fair," Brenda commented.

"What wasn't fair was that Kumar should have been the first author on the paper. That position goes to the person who did the most work. Larramore put himself as first author. I think Kumar was very annoyed."

"Would not being first author damage his job prospects?" Brenda asked.

"I hope not. Kumar deserves a very good academic position. If our department were hiring this year, I'd recruit him myself. He's always complaining that his parents want him to come back to India and get married. Unfortunately, there aren't any prestigious astronomy departments in India, and he's been living here too long to marry a stranger his mother has selected for him.

"How will Dr. Larramore's death affect Kumar's career?" Daniel asked.

"I don't know. Departments look carefully at strong letters of recommendation from one's advisor."

"Now that Dr. Larramore is deceased, what will happen to his Nobel Prize? Will they award it to someone else?" Daniel asked.

Wilson shook his head. "They've already made the announcement. Nobel Prizes aren't awarded posthumously, but if a recipient dies between the announcement in October and the Prize ceremony in December, he still gets it. That's happened just three times that I'm aware of."

"What happens to the money?" Brenda asked.

"I assume it will go to Larramore's heirs, most likely his wife," Wilson said.

"Is it a large amount?" Daniel asked.

"Over a million dollars this year," Wilson said. "The amount is based on the yearly interest earned by the fund, so it varies."

"Are there rules on how a recipient can spend it?" Brenda asked.

Wilson shook his head. "Most prize winners either donate the money to charity, or use it to fund their research, but there's nothing to prevent a winner from buying a Ferrari."

"Interesting," Brenda said.

"How was your work relationship with Larramore?" Daniel asked. "Did you two get along?"

Wilson shrugged. "I interacted primarily with his students," he said. "Larramore was rather aloof, not much of a team player."

"Did the two of you socialize at all? Lunch? Dinner?" Brenda asked.

"Not really," Wilson said. "I'd go out for beers with the students, but he never joined us."

"I'm sure you've heard that we've classified his death a homicide," Daniel said. "We're asking all his close colleagues for an account of their whereabouts on Friday, and on Saturday morning."

"Friday was the symposium. I was there all day along with his students. After the conference, I went back to my apartment. Saturday morning, I went to the Institute's gym at about eight o'clock and worked out for an hour. I didn't hear about Dr. Larramore's death until later in the afternoon, when George Tayler phoned to tell us all."

"Can you think of anyone who might have had a reason to kill him?" Daniel asked.

Wilson shook his head. "He wasn't the nicest guy on the block. Most of his students seemed intimidated by him. But I can't think of anyone who would want to kill him. I only know the students and faculty who were involved with him. I know nothing about his personal life. It's possible your answer lies there, Detectives."

"Perhaps," Daniel said. "Thank you for your time."

"That was one cool customer," Brenda said as they walked toward the elevator. "Have you noticed how every time we interview one of these guys, we get a lecture on astronomy? Even if we never solve the murder, we'll know more about extrasolar planets than anyone else in the LAPD."

"For all the good that does us," Daniel commented. "But maybe his suggestion was correct. Perhaps we are looking at the wrong group of people. Maybe this murder has a motive that has nothing to do with academics."

"Maybe the motive is the prize money. Over a million is nothing to sneeze at," Brenda said. "If his wife is his heir, she could have killed him so she would get to spend the big bucks."

"I don't buy it," Daniel said. "Think about the timing. She didn't find out he'd won the Prize until early Saturday morning. He died before he even knew. I don't think the prize money is the motive."

"Do you have an alternative?" Brenda asked.

"Sometimes the most reputable people have secret lives," Daniel said. "We just need to keep probing his life until we uncover something. I'll get the guys started on his finances tomorrow, and you and I will see who shows up at the memorial service."

CHAPTER TWELVE

I HAD SCHEDULED MY DAY AROUND THE 4:00 P.M. memorial service at the Institute. I was wearing a dark gray pantsuit, appropriate for both the office and the event. I'd always been fond of Carolyn, who had been my patient for many years. About a year after her marriage, Carolyn had come in to consult with me about pregnancy. She hadn't been using birth control, and yet nothing had happened.

I had taken her through the first steps of a standard infertility workup and couldn't find anything wrong. The one missing piece of data was a sperm count. Carolyn had said that Edwin refused to have one done, convinced that if she wasn't getting pregnant, it was obviously her fault. This had not impressed me.

In my experience, men who refused to participate in an infertility work-up had no real interest in having children. Now that Carolyn had shared her true feelings about her husband, things were making sense.

I was actually surprised when Carolyn became pregnant and had hoped, at the time, that my intuition about Edwin had been wrong. I had never met him. Unlike most husbands, he never accompanied his wife to an obstetrical appointment, and now, of course, he never would.

The memorial service took place in the largest auditorium of the Physics and Astronomy building, and a large crowd of somberly dressed people were already milling about the corridor when I arrived. I spotted Carolyn, along with two older couples, greeting people as they filed into the room. I signed the guest book, thinking that Daniel would probably want a copy of it, and took my place in line.

"Dr. Kline. Thank you so much for coming." Carolyn's face was pale and her expression was tense, but she managed a smile and hugged me. "Please come to the house afterwards," she said.

"Of course, I will."

I proceeded into the auditorium, scanning the crowd for a sign of Daniel or Brenda. I spotted them coming in a side entrance, bypassing the crowd outside, and seating themselves in the last row. Daniel noticed me, and acknowledged my presence with a discreet smile.

The memorial was about what I had expected. One of the older men at Carolyn's side turned out to be the department chairman, and he opened the proceedings with praise for Edwin Larramore's outstanding contributions to astronomy. He was followed by a series of colleagues, all of whom shared stories of scientific achievement. There didn't seem to be any truly personal stories that would have shed light on Edwin's character. It was all very professional.

At the end of the service, friends and family were invited to the Larramore's home, and the crowd filed out and scattered. I picked up the flyer with the address and directions and decided to walk. The house was only a few blocks from campus. Daniel and Brenda seem to have left already and I was pretty certain they would not be at the home reception. It would be up to me to see if I could glean a few tidbits that I could ethically share.

CHAPTER THIRTEEN

After the memorial, Daniel sent Brenda home and returned to the station to gather his thoughts. The morning team meeting had not yielded any new suspects, despite interviews with all the faculty of the Physics, Astronomy and Chemistry departments. No one had been willing to bad-mouth the dead, especially the dead Nobel Prize winner, but the sum total of all the interviews had painted a fairly clear picture of Edwin Larramore's character. He was brilliant, hard-working, demanding, competitive and not at all social. No one claimed to be his friend, or even an occasional dinner guest. It seemed clear that he was respected but not liked. Most of the Chemistry faculty had never met him, but had kind words for Carolyn. Her colleagues described her as smart, friendly, collaborative and very popular with students. A few of the women faculty had often joined her for lunch, but could shed no light on the marriage.

The one bright spot was that the team had managed to trace one of the authors of the chemistry paper about the poison. Professor William McKenzie, former chairman of the Chemistry Department at UC San Diego, and author of hundreds of chemistry papers, had retired about ten years ago, but still lived close to the university, in a residential neighborhood called La Jolla Shores. J.C. Neuman, the other author, had vanished without a trace. There were no further scientific papers under his name, no driver's license, tax return, death certificate or police record. Daniel left that mystery for further contemplation and phoned Dr. McKenzie. He explained that he needed the doctor's scientific expertise to help with a police case, and asked if he could come down and interview him. Experience had taught Daniel that trying to interview an elderly person over the phone could be frustrating. Besides, the thought of going down to La Jolla was a pleasant one. The professor agreed to see Daniel the next day, Saturday, and he called Hannah to see if she and Zoe would like to spend the weekend exploring La Jolla.

Hannah was on her way to the Larramore house when he called. "Absolutely," she said. "Is the LAPD picking up the hotel tab?"

"Dream on," Daniel said. "But since I have to interview someone from the University, I thought it was a great opportunity to combine business with pleasure. You can take Zoe to the beach while I'm doing my interview."

"Perfect. I can pack as soon as I get home. I won't stay long at the Larramore's, but Carolyn specifically asked me to come, and I feel as if I should lend her some support."

"I'll head home, relieve Emilia, and entertain Zoe until you get back," Daniel said. "See you later."

Daniel booked a room at a Best Western Hotel in La Jolla Cove and, smiling to himself, finished writing his notes for the day and left the station.

CHAPTER FOURTEEN

I ENJOYED MY BRISK WALK IN THE COOL EVENING AIR, and noticing the lack of street parking near the Larramore's house, decided that walking had been the right decision. The house was a charming, old, Spanish Revival, on a knoll, with a winding staircase leading to the front door. All the house lights were on, the door was open, and people were crowded into the large, high-beamed living room.

A fire was burning in the Spanish tile fireplace, and a large group surrounded the dining room table, where a lavish buffet was laid out. This was what my partner Ruth always referred to as "deli after death," the consumption of food and drink to drown one's sorrows and return to a semblance of normal life.

I didn't recognize anyone in the crowd. I have always hated going to receptions or meetings where I know none of the participants. Working a room is not one of my talents and I always feel shy about initiating a conversation with a stranger. This posed a particular challenge since I was hoping to pick up information here that people might be reluctant to share with the police. It was different in the office, where I met strangers every day. The nature of the conversation had well-defined rules, and I was in charge.

Stepping back into the corridor, I looked for a place to hang my coat.

"Everyone's throwing them in the spare bedroom," a voice said.

I turned my head and spotted a tall, elegant woman, in a beautifully tailored black suit, wearing a large pair of tortoise shell glasses. She had thick black hair, with a single gray streak, and wore bright red lipstick. "Here, let me show you."

She led me down the hall to a small room with a wrought iron bedstead, piled high with coats.

"Thanks. I'm Hannah Kline, by the way."

The woman held out her hand and I shook it. "Isobel Martin. So, are you a physicist, astronomer, chemist or spouse?" she asked.

"None of the above," I said. "I'm a physician. Yourself?"

"Astronomer," Isobel said. "I was in town for the conference when Edwin died, and decided I should stay for the memorial."

"That was kind of you," I said. "Were you close colleagues?"

"We were fierce competitors," Isobel said. "We used to be married."

"Then it's doubly kind of you to be here," I said.

"What about you? How did you know my ex?" Isobel asked.

"I didn't know him," I said. "I'm Carolyn's obstetrician and I'm very fond of her. I wanted to pay my respects."

Isobel shook her head. "Amazing. When we were married, Edwin was completely uninterested in children. I wonder what she did to change his mind. Come on, let's get a drink." She tucked her arm into mine and steered me in the direction of the bar in the den.

Drinks in hand, scotch for Isobel and a white wine for me, we found two chairs next to a coffee table with crackers and hummus.

"It feels good to sit down," I said. "I don't really know anyone here, so it's a little difficult to circulate."

"I know lots of people here," Isobel said. "And I'd just as soon not talk to any of them. All anyone has been discussing all week is the unanswerable question of who murdered Edwin. Have the police said how he was killed?"

I shook my head. "I haven't heard anything. I believe they are keeping that information to themselves at the moment. There hasn't been anything in the media. Do you have any idea of who might have wanted to kill him?"

Isobel shrugged. "Probably a cast of thousands. When we were married, I wanted to kill him myself on a daily basis. He was such a shit. I finally got over it after the divorce."

She took a deep swallow of her scotch and let out a sigh of satisfaction.

"What did he do?" I asked.

"The last year we were married, we both finished our PhD's and started looking for jobs. He simply assumed that I would follow him wherever he landed and take some second-class position, because he saw himself as a junior Einstein to whom everyone else must defer. When I got an offer from Columbia and refused to turn it down, he went ballistic. He was so angry, he actually hit me and stormed out of the apartment. I packed a suitcase and checked into a hotel before he came back. The next day, I found a divorce lawyer. No way in hell was I going to be an abused wife."

"That's quite a story," I said. "I'm doubly surprised that you'd want to attend his memorial."

"Hold that thought," Isobel said.

She stood up and got a refill on her scotch.

"Academic politics," she said. "Our two groups are the leading competitors in the search for extrasolar planets. We simultaneously developed and published the transit method for detecting them, although Edwin always behaved as if it was his unique idea. He had a galactic-sized ego. Anyway, it would look bad if I didn't pay my respects. Besides, Carolyn's a nice woman. I feel sorry for her."

"Do you think he abused her?" I asked.

Isobel shrugged. "He may not have needed to resort to physical abuse if she was appropriately subordinate and obedient. There are other ways to control a wife."

This was certainly food for thought. "Will you be in town for much longer?" I asked. Daniel would certainly want to know.

"I'm leaving on Monday. Thought I'd enjoy the weather over the weekend and visit with a few LA friends," she said.

"Isobel, how nice to see you." A tall, dark-haired, Asian, professorial-type man approached us and leaned over to kiss Isobel on her cheek.

I used the interlude to get up. "I'm afraid I have to go. I have a daughter to feed and I'm expected home. Do you know where Carolyn is? I want to see her before I leave. It's been really nice meeting you."

"Kitchen, last I looked," the professorial-type said.

"Thanks," I said, as he slid into my vacated chair.

∼

There was a large crowd in the kitchen, but I eventually spotted Carolyn near the coffee maker and made my way over.

"Dr. Kline, I'm glad you made it."

"Are you okay?" I asked. "You seem to have a great many friends here."

She shrugged. "Mostly colleagues. I'm holding it together. I wanted to take you up on your offer. You said I could come in, if I just wanted to talk, even if it wasn't time for my regular appointment."

"Of course, you can. Why don't you pick an afternoon and come after I finish with my patients? That way, we'll have as much time as you need to talk. I'll let the front desk know that you'll be calling."

"Thanks," she said. "I'll try to come in next week."

An elderly man touched her shoulder and Carolyn turned away to speak to him. I began to slowly wend my way through the crowd, so that I could retrieve my coat. As I squeezed through the arched doorway, I bumped into a familiar-looking woman with ash blonde hair.

"Hannah, I didn't expect to run into you here." It was Jackie, my realtor.

"Ditto," I said. "I had no idea you knew the Larramores. Did you find them this wonderful house?"

"Actually, I did," she said, "but that's not why I'm here. Carolyn is my daughter."

CHAPTER FIFTEEN

DANIEL HAD GOTTEN HOME BEFORE ME, AND HE AND Zoe were in the kitchen, tossing salad.

"Emilia and I baked cookies, Mommy," Zoe announced.

"Fantastic," I said, depositing a kiss on her forehead and one on Daniel's cheek. "It smells great in here."

A tray of chocolate chip cookies was cooling on the counter, and my determination to cut carbs rapidly disappeared with the scent.

"We made beef stew for dinner, too," Zoe announced. "And I'm finished with all my homework."

"You are a wonder," I said. "Let me wash my hands, set the table and we can eat."

"Did you have an interesting time at the reception?" Daniel asked, as he handed me the silverware.

"Very," I said. "I spent most of my time talking with Isobel Martin, Edwin Larramore's ex-wife. I'll tell you the details later, but you might want to know that she'll be in town until Monday. Is that going to mess up our La Jolla weekend? I know you need to interview her."

"Sounds like a job for my trusted right hand," Daniel

said. "Let me call Brenda right now and have her track Dr. Martin down. You're right. We should speak to her before she flies back east."

"Great idea," I said. "I'm looking forward to La Jolla."

After dinner, I sent Zoe to her room and told her what to pack for the weekend. Over the dinner dishes, I updated Daniel on my conversation with Isobel.

"You have no idea how helpful that is," Daniel said. "Everyone we interviewed has referred to him as only slightly less holy than God. I've had the feeling all along that people were hiding their real opinions. So, the guy was a bastard?"

"Seems like it," I said.

"Do you think he abused Carolyn?" Daniel asked.

I paused, pouring detergent into the dishwasher. "Daniel, you know that even if I knew, I couldn't tell you. Carolyn is my patient."

"Sorry, honey," Daniel said. "On another topic, when do your parents get in?"

"Thanksgiving morning. I'll pick them up. They can't wait to meet you."

"I'm looking forward to meeting them too," Daniel said.

I took a deep breath. Despite their skill at aggravating me, my parents had always been supportive and I'd relied on their constant visits and calls during the year after Ben's death. I did, however, have some trepidation about this meeting.

"I should warn you," I said. "Mom can be a little intrusive. She won't hesitate to ask all kinds of questions about when we're getting married and what kind of wedding are we planning. That's why I waited to tell them about our engagement. She doesn't understand why we're buying a house together before we tie the knot."

"What kind of a wedding are we planning and why are we buying a house first?" Daniel asked, grinning at me.

I rolled my eyes at him. "I can only handle one major stressor at a time," I said. "It's easier to buy a house and move, because we only have to please ourselves. Once we start planning a wedding, we're going to get input from both our families and we won't be able to please everyone."

"What kind of a wedding would please you?" Daniel asked.

We hadn't really talked much about weddings. Once we were living together and I was wearing Daniel's ring, there didn't seem to be any rush.

"A small one," I said. "Immediate family and best friends. We've both been married before. I don't need to walk down the aisle in a wedding gown again."

"Do you want a religious ceremony?" Daniel asked.

That was the elephant in the room. I hadn't mentioned to my parents that Daniel wasn't Jewish, and I was prepared for some unwanted advice once they found out. Daniel's parents were pillars of the Millbrae Episcopal Church, and no doubt assumed that Daniel was marrying into the fold. I was anxious to avoid any discussion of religious differences at either parental end. In all the time Daniel and I had been together, the subject had never come up.

"Definitely not," I said. "Neither of us is religious and finding a rabbi or a minister willing to do a non-denominational, mixed marriage would be a huge chore. That's probably the part where both sets of parents will want to weigh in, and they'll make us crazy."

I could see the relief on his face at my answer.

"You're right about that," Daniel said. "I just thought we should discuss it, so we're on the same page, if your parents ask."

"You mean when my parents ask," I said. "By the way, I forgot to mention one other thing. I ran into our realtor, Jackie, at the reception. It turns out that she's Carolyn's mother. I'm wondering if that could be a problem."

"Does she know what I do for a living?" Daniel asked.

"I don't think I ever mentioned it, but it would be awkward if Carolyn found out I was engaged to the guy who's solving her husband's murder."

"You may need to go house hunting without me for awhile," he said. "

I nodded and started the dishwasher. I wondered if there was any helpful information I could extract from Jackie for Daniel. After all, she wasn't my patient. Confidentiality didn't apply.

"We'd better go upstairs and pack a few things for the weekend," I said.

CHAPTER SIXTEEN

S INCE DANIEL HAD TO BE IN LA JOLLA BY NOON, AT THE latest, they left right after breakfast and reached La Jolla at 10:30 a.m. It was too early to check into their hotel, so they parked the car and walked along the shore to the children's beach, which had been taken over by a large colony of seals.

This had caused considerable uproar in the community, but ultimately, the tourist attraction won out and people were banned from the beach. Spring was the best time, when the newborns were frolicking on the sand, but Zoe was still fascinated by being so close to the adult seals.

Daniel watched Zoe with a smile. When he and Annie had been married, he'd cooperated with her desire to have children, but truthfully, he'd had no strong passion to be a father, so he wasn't as disappointed as she was when she failed to become pregnant. But, perhaps his ambivalence had more to do with Annie than with parenthood.

Zoe had been a revelation. He still marveled at how quickly he had bonded to her, and how she could erase the effects of his stressful days with her enchanting smile. He'd even begun to wonder if Hannah would consider having another child. She was thirty-eight and he was forty-three. Was that too old?

At 11:30 a.m., Daniel left them taking photos with Hannah's phone and drove to the McKenzie home on El Paseo Grande, in La Jolla Shores. It was a modest, one-story house. The doorbell was answered by an elderly man using a walker. Professor McKenzie was tall and thin, dressed in a neatly-pressed, light blue shirt and khaki pants, and wearing leather bedroom slippers. His face was tanned, wrinkled and weathered, with sparkling blue eyes, and his scalp was bald and freckled. Daniel had researched the professor's curriculum vitae before coming and knew that he had just celebrated his 90th birthday. He hoped that Dr. McKenzie's mind was as alert as his smile.

Dr. McKenzie held out a hand, carefully holding on to his walker with the other, and Daniel shook it. Turning, the professor shuffled toward the back of the house, motioning to Daniel to follow. The back room was a stunning wall of windows, looking out onto a small deck and the beach. Surfers were gliding over the waves in the distance and sea gulls were pecking at the seaweed on the sand.

"You like it?" McKenzie asked.

"Gorgeous," Daniel said.

"My wife and I bought it in the seventies, when I joined the faculty. No professor could afford it today. I love sitting here in the morning and watching the waves. Have a seat."

Daniel seated himself in one of two comfortable leather armchairs facing the view. There was a table between them with a thermos, some cream and sugar, and two UCSD coffee mugs.

"Have some coffee," McKenzie said, pouring for both of

them. "And tell me how I can help you. It's been a long time since someone asked my scientific advice. I'm a bit rusty."

Daniel removed a folder out of his briefcase and handed McKenzie a copy of his paper. "This is a paper you published forty-five years ago, with J.C. Neuman, on a substance called Nickel Diarsine. Do you remember it?"

McKenzie nodded. "I do. Why are you interested in it?"

Daniel had decided that if he really wanted help, he was going to have to be honest about his reasons.

"This is confidential," he said, "but I'm investigating a homicide in which Nickel Diarsine was used to poison the victim. I need to know something about it. How would someone get hold of it or make it, and why would they choose that particular poison?"

McKenzie's eyebrows rose. "It is a strange choice," he said. "It's quite obscure and you can't obtain it without synthesizing it."

"Would that be difficult?" Daniel asked.

"It's not something you could do in your kitchen. The fumes are extremely toxic. You'd need a hood with good ventilation, such as the ones we have in our labs. You could purchase the precursor ingredients from chemical supply houses, but I don't understand why anyone would go to the trouble. There are lots of toxic substances that are much easier to obtain."

"Perhaps the substance has some special significance for the killer," Daniel said. "I tried to read your paper, but the mathematics completely stymied me. What is the substance used for? Why were you studying it?"

"As far as I know, it has no commercial use. We were looking at it because of its unusual electronic properties. Its structure, a nickel atom in the middle, surrounded by four arsenics, was able to stabilize an unusual electronic state.

Nickel usually has a charge of +2 when it is combined with other atoms. In this compound it's +3, which is highly unusual. We looked at the spectra and replicated them with quantum mechanical calculations."

"It must have been quite a difficult piece of research," Daniel said.

"I can't take the credit," McKenzie said. "The project was my idea and I supervised it, but my graduate student did all the work and wrote the paper."

"We've tried to trace J.C. Neuman without any luck," Daniel said. "He doesn't seem to have published anything after this paper."

McKenzie smiled. "You mean she. Jaycee was one of my smartest students, and the only woman at the time. Despite an excellent thesis, she was never able to find a job in academic chemistry. It was something of an old boys' club back then and there weren't many good jobs available. I don't know what happened to her. I heard she and her husband moved back East. I imagine she left chemistry and did something else."

"So," Daniel said. "If you were looking for someone with access to this compound, where would you look?"

"I'd certainly look for a chemist, or a friend of one, or for someone with access to a lab with a hood. It still seems like a very peculiar choice of murder weapon," he added.

Daniel phoned Hannah as soon as he was done with the interview. They met back at the hotel, where they checked in and changed. Hannah dressed in a long beach cover up, slathered herself in more sun block, and put on a wide brimmed hat. Redheads and sun didn't mix well.

Zoe put on her bathing suit and collected all her beach toys. They drove to Avenida de la Playa, bought sandwiches and drinks at the La Jolla Cheese Shop, and with beach towels and chairs, in hand, picnicked on the beach. Hannah and Daniel read on their twin Kindles, keeping a careful eye on Zoe, who was making sand castles. They took turns walking her down to the ocean, so she could test the temperature for herself, but November was way too cold without a wet suit. They returned in the late afternoon, showered and changed and went out to Spice and Rice for a family Thai dinner.

As they were working their way through the Mee Krob, Brenda phoned. The restaurant was noisy so Daniel took the call outside.

"Did you track her down?" Daniel asked.

"I did. That is one tough cookie," Brenda said.

"What did you find out?"

"Hannah already told you that he was a bastard. They've been divorced for over twenty years. Now they only fight in astronomy journals. Apparently, their two groups have discovered the largest number of extrasolar planets. They also simultaneously discovered and published a method for finding smaller planets. I had the sense she was just a bit jealous that he'd gotten a Nobel and she hadn't."

"What about an alibi?" Daniel asked.

"We're checking the details, but she claims to have been at the conference all day Friday. She gave a lecture and did an afternoon workshop, so that should be easy to confirm."

"Did she have any private conversations with her ex?" Daniel asked.

"She claims that, other than a brief handshake in public, she had no contact with Edwin that day. They apparently avoid one another. I'm getting the security tapes from her hotel to see when she returned on Friday night and what time she left on Saturday morning. At the moment, I don't see how she could have gotten into Edwin's office unless he left it unlocked during the day."

"Okay, thanks," Daniel said. "Anything else?"

"There's one other very interesting point that we'll need to follow up on when you get back. Isobel told me she was surprised to see that Carolyn was pregnant. She said Edwin had been very clear during their marriage that he disliked children and had absolutely no desire to have one of his own. Apparently, he acted on his convictions. I just got the final autopsy report from Bill Pincus. Larramore had a vasectomy. Unless it was a very badly done procedure, he couldn't be the father of Carolyn's child."

CHAPTER SEVENTEEN

WHEN DANIEL RETURNED FROM HIS PHONE CALL, I could tell he had something on his mind.

"Everything okay?" I asked.

He nodded and dug into his soup.

After dinner, we strolled around the cove and returned to the hotel. The three of us watched an "on demand" animated movie and then tucked Zoe into her bed. We couldn't really talk without waking her, let alone make love, so we read in bed until we were drowsy enough to turn off the reading lights.

It occurred to me that we were overdue for a romantic weekend. I felt some nostalgia for the days when he still had his Venice bungalow and we could go there for privacy and great sex.

It wasn't until we returned home on Sunday and were alone in our bedroom that Daniel posed a medical question.

"Theoretically," he said, "if you saw a couple who wanted to get pregnant, and the husband had a vasectomy, what alternatives would they have?"

I raised my eyebrows. "Well, vasectomies can be

reversed, although the results aren't guaranteed. It's a delicate microsurgical procedure. The couple can also use a sperm bank. In my experience, most men avoid vasectomies and leave birth control to their wives, even though tying off a woman's fallopian tubes is a much bigger deal. I think there's something about being operated on 'down there' that freaks them out."

Daniel smiled. "What do you think might motivate a man with no children to have a vasectomy?"

"Why are you asking?" Was he thinking of having one?

"I'm just picking your medical brain about a case."

I had, of course, immediately taken care of birth control as soon as Daniel and I became lovers. It would be rather embarrassing if I had an accident. Why then, I wondered, did I feel a sense of relief to know that a personal vasectomy wasn't on his mind? I hadn't really thought about a second child, but maybe it wasn't out of the question.

"I would think that the only reason to do that would be if a man was absolutely certain he never wanted children, or wanted to avoid passing on a genetic abnormality."

I was beginning to suspect we were talking about Edwin Larramore, but I didn't really want to know.

CHAPTER EIGHTEEN

THE SUBJECT OF EDWIN LARRAMORE'S VASECTOMY WAS first on the agenda during the Monday morning team meeting. Daniel was feeling more than a little frustrated. If Carolyn had used a sperm bank, Hannah would know, but Daniel couldn't ask her. If she had a lover, Edwin would have known immediately that the child wasn't his. Had he accused her or abused her when he found out? Had Carolyn even known that her husband was sterile? There was only one person Daniel could ask. It was clearly time for another interview with the widowed Dr. Larramore.

Daniel and Brenda found Carolyn in her laboratory. She was wearing a white coat, a pair of goggles, a mask and latex gloves, and carefully pipetting a solution into a series of culture tubes. She looked up, surprised to see them, and motioned for them to stay where they were.

"I'll be with you in a moment. I need to finish and refrigerate these tubes. I don't want to risk any contamination."

They waited until she was done, and had discarded her gloves, mask and goggles.

"Can we have a word, Dr. Larramore?" Daniel asked politely. "There's some new information we need to ask you about."

"Let's go to my office. It's just next door."

Carolyn's office was bright and cheerful with large windows, full bookcases and contemporary art on the walls. There were two comfortable chairs across from her desk and she asked them to have a seat.

"What have you learned?" she asked.

"Your husband's autopsy is complete," Daniel said. "Can you tell us when he had his vasectomy?"

"His what?" Carolyn's jaw dropped and her face flushed. "That's impossible."

Her hands reached for the bulge of her pregnancy.

"He never said anything about a vasectomy," she said. "All the time we were trying to get pregnant he never said one word. It must not have been a very successful vasectomy. I got pregnant anyway."

"Did you have any difficulty getting pregnant?" Daniel asked.

"I had some infertility testing. It took over a year before I got pregnant," Caroline said.

Brenda looked at her sympathetically. "Are you certain this is your husband's child?" she asked. Brenda did "good cop" very well.

"Who else's would it be?" Carolyn said.

"That's what we'd like to know," Daniel said. "Did you use a sperm bank, Dr. Larramore?"

"No, absolutely not!"

Carolyn was clearly unsettled and angry. It also seemed to Daniel that she was lying. Time to push harder.

"Do you have a lover?" he asked.

Her face flushed again and she stood up. "I think it's time for you to leave my office, Detectives."

"What's your take?" Daniel asked Brenda.

"I think she was genuinely surprised at the news her husband had a vasectomy, but I think she definitely has a lover."

"Agreed. It's looking more likely than ever that she, or perhaps her lover, is the murderer. She certainly has the skills and technology to create the chemical, and if her lover is the father of her child, that provides a strong motive. Perhaps the two of them collaborated."

"So, what's our next step?" Brenda asked.

"Dr. McKenzie gave me a list of ingredients essential for synthesizing the arsenic compound. I'll get the team to check every chemical supply house in Southern California, beginning with the ones routinely used by the Chemistry department. Hopefully, the results of that investigation will enable me to get a search warrant for Carolyn Larramore's laboratory and home," Daniel said.

"Any brilliant ideas for tracking down her lover?" Brenda asked.

"Not at the moment, but I'm sure I'll think of something," Daniel said, with a sigh.

This was one of those situations where Hannah would have been invaluable. In their time together, her insights and connections had helped him to solve three murder cases. However, in each case, Hannah had known the victim and had a personal stake in the solution. This case was different. Hannah didn't know the victim and was bound by patient confidentiality in her care of his wife. It was a shame.

CHAPTER NINETEEN

T HE FIRST THING I NOTICED, WHEN I CHECKED MY office schedule for Tuesday, was that Carolyn Larramore had wasted no time in getting an appointment. She was my last patient of the day, which meant that my hopes for getting out early, and finishing my Thanksgiving shopping on my way home, were dashed.

I was beginning to regret my offer to talk further with her, which I had made prior to learning that her husband's death was a homicide. The whole situation was making me uncomfortable. For one thing, I didn't want to revisit my own pregnancy after Ben's death. It had been a horribly painful time, and I had no sage advice to offer Carolyn to make her time any better. In addition, the situations were not the same. I had been very much in love with Ben, and she had been struggling with deciding to leave her husband.

I had lots of good tips for surviving single motherhood, but Carolyn wasn't there yet. Finally, I was a gynecologist, not a psychotherapist. Perhaps the most useful thing I could accomplish this afternoon was to refer her to my best friend Andrea, who was a superbly talented psychiatrist.

Having settled on a plan of action, I pulled a chart from the nearest exam room door and went inside to see my first patient.

When Carolyn was ushered into my consult room late that afternoon, she seemed agitated and looked unkempt. She was wearing jeans and an old T-shirt. Her eyes were puffy, as if she'd been crying, and she wore no make-up. Even her hair was wild, as if she'd been running her fingers through it.

I smiled at her warmly and motioned for her to sit down. "How are you holding up?"

"Not well. I've had some upsetting news and I need to ask you a medical question. This is completely confidential, right?"

"Of course," I assured her.

"The police came yesterday. They told me that Edwin had had a vasectomy. They were quite positive about it."

"You had no idea?" I asked. So that explained Daniel's medical questions.

"Of course not. I spent a year timing my ovulations so I could get pregnant. Why would I do that if I knew he had been sterilized? Is there any way to tell when he had the surgery? Either he did it after I got pregnant, or somehow, the procedure failed. Is that possible? How could the bastard get sterilized without telling me?"

"That's more than one question," I said. "I seem to remember that Edwin refused to have a sperm count when we were investigating why you were having trouble conceiving. Is it possible he refused because he knew it would show no sperm?"

"You're suggesting he just pretended he was willing to have children, knowing the whole time that we wouldn't?"

"That's one possibility," I said.

"What are the others?"

"If he had the vasectomy very shortly before you became pregnant, there might still have been sperm in the pipeline. Or, he could have decided he didn't want children and had it, not knowing you were already pregnant."

Carolyn ran her fingers through her hair again. "Is there any way I can find out when he had it done?"

"If you're the executor of his will, you could obtain his medical records. The vasectomy would be part of his medical history. If he has a urologist, and you know who it is, there should be an operative report with a date."

I watched as she bit her lip and clasped and unclasped her hands.

"What if he had it a long time ago? Could this still be his child?"

"Is there another possibility?" I asked.

She nodded. "I developed a close friendship, months ago, with a visiting professor. We started having coffee together in the morning, then lunch. One afternoon, I went to his apartment and we made love. I can't say I felt guilty about it. He was much more affectionate than Edwin ever was. It was just once."

"Did you end it?" I asked.

"I broke it off because it was too risky for both of us. If Edwin found out, he'd have ruined Oliver's career. I never suspected, until now, that Edwin wasn't the father of my baby. We'd had sex that month right on ovulation day, four days after I'd been with Oliver. "

Women didn't realize that sperm could last four or five

days in the fallopian tubes. "If you want to know, we could do a paternity test with Edwin's DNA."

"I don't know if I want to know. I don't know if I want to tell Oliver. I'll consider getting the medical records. Then I'll decide."

This was getting too complicated for me. Daniel would love to have this information but there was too much conflict of interest.

I took a deep breath. "Carolyn, do you think it might help for you to talk to a therapist who could help you to sort this out? I can recommend an excellent psychiatrist, if you'd like."

She sat there, chewing her lip again. "That sounds like it might be a good idea. I'll take a name if you have one."

I scribbled Andrea's name and phone number onto a prescription pad and handed it to her. She put it in her purse and rose.

"Happy Thanksgiving, Doc," she said. "And thanks."

CHAPTER TWENTY

As soon as Carolyn left, I called Daniel, firmly repressing my impulse to tell him what I knew.

"Hi, sweetie. I'm leaving the office and heading for the supermarket. I'll be home a little late. I've got to do all the Thanksgiving shopping I didn't have time for this weekend."

"Why don't I give Zoe her dinner, see if Emilia can stay late, and take you out for an adult meal, after we've unpacked the groceries? I'm in the mood for Italian," Daniel said.

The thought of being waited on was very appealing, and we wouldn't have any alone time over the holiday weekend while my parents were visiting.

"Great idea," I said.

Daniel met me in our garage and helped carry ten bags of turkey, sweet potatoes, cranberries, and all the other fixings upstairs. I put one more thing on the list for my dream house. I wanted a garage on the same level as the kitchen.

I went in and kissed Zoe hello.

"Thanks for babysitting, Emilia," I said. "Daniel and I will be home no later than nine."

"You go, now," she said. "I take care of the groceries."

"You're a gem," I said.

We went to Pizzicotto, our favorite neighborhood Italian restaurant. It was small, unpretentious and had great food. It also had a quiet and private upstairs, with only a few tables. Daniel had had the foresight to call and reserve one. I noticed only two other couples dining upstairs, at the other end of the room. With a sigh of relaxation, I sat down and began dipping Italian olive bread into a mixture of olive oil, balsamic vinegar, herbs and garlic.

The waiter came upstairs and delivered two glasses of red wine to one of the other tables before coming to take our order. I asked for a Pinot Grigio and Daniel ordered Chianti.

I glanced across the room. At one of the other tables, two women, dressed in jeans and leather jackets, were seated together. The one facing me had a narrow face, dark hair, a pixie haircut and a camel-colored jacket with large zippers. The one with her back to me was wearing royal blue leather, which contrasted nicely with her shoulder-length blonde hair.

The women leaned toward one another, held hands and toasted with their red wine. The blonde turned slightly to her left and I realized she looked familiar.

"Daniel," I whispered. "Isn't that Brenda at the table behind you?"

Daniel ventured a quick look and nodded. The two women were leaning in, toward one another, still holding hands. The expression on the brunette's face didn't strike me as the sort of look you give your best girlfriend. It was more of a sultry, *let's go to bed right after dinner* look.

"Should we go over and say hello?" he said.

"I think not. They look like they don't want company."

"You know, Brenda's been unusually cheerful lately. I've been wondering if there's someone new in her life."

"Did you ever suspect she was a lesbian?"

"I never gave it any thought," Daniel said. "It's hard enough to be a woman at the LAPD. I wouldn't be surprised if she decided keep her private life private, even to me."

The waiter arrived with two large plates of pasta for Brenda's table, and shortly thereafter, whitefish with pistachio crust for me, and Osso Bucco for Daniel. We dug into a satisfying meal.

Brenda and her companion finished before we did, and as they got up to leave, Brenda spotted me. I saw a slight flush on her cheeks.

"Hannah, nice to see you," she said, regaining her composure.

Daniel smiled at her.

I gave her a surprised look. "Brenda, hi. I didn't notice you," I said. "I like the jacket."

"Thanks," Brenda said. "This is my friend Marcy. Marcy meet Daniel Ross, my partner at LAPD, and his fiancée, Hannah Kline."

Daniel rose and he and Marcy shook hands.

"Have you eaten here before?" she asked. "The food's really good."

Daniel nodded. "It's one of our regular neighborhood places. Glad you enjoyed it. We were trying to have a relaxing adult meal before Hannah's parents arrive from the East Coast."

Brenda smiled. "I know what you mean. I'm having

Thanksgiving dinner with my family in West Covina, assuming no one else gets murdered on our watch."

Daniel grinned. "No work talk tonight," he said. "I'll see you tomorrow. Nice to meet you, Marcy."

The two women walked down the stairs.

"Do you think she'll say anything to you tomorrow?" I asked.

"Knowing Brenda, probably not," Daniel said. "It's too bad. I wish she would realize that she can trust me for more than just watching her back when we go after killers."

CHAPTER TWENTY-ONE

"W HAT WOULD I DO WITHOUT GOOGLE?" THE comment came from Izzy, otherwise known as Isidore Washington, the Detective Squad's reigning computer whiz kid.

Izzy had grown up in South Central, had managed to avoid being recruited into a gang, and had majored in computer science at Cal State L.A. He was a skinny guy, with a two-inch Afro, gold wire-rimmed glasses and very prominent ears. Daniel had always been grateful that Izzy had decided to join the LAPD instead of going to work for some company in Silicon Valley.

"What did you find?" Daniel asked. He grabbed a stale chocolate doughnut from the box he had brought for the Monday morning meeting. Hannah would probably not approve.

"Well, I concentrated on the arsenic compound needed for the synthesis, as it was the most specific. There are four manufacturers of research chemicals that make it, but three of them are in China. The one in the US is in Massachusetts. You can purchase five grams for $137."

Izzy followed in Daniel's footsteps and grabbed the last of the jelly doughnuts. "I called and asked if they could check their purchase records for the past ten years, and send them to me, without a search warrant. And they did. Unfortunately, there was very little information to share. Phenylene-bis-dimethyl-arsine isn't exactly a best seller. They had only a handful of orders over the past ten years, and most of them were out of the country." He handed Daniel a printout of the information. "I don't think this is going to help you much."

Daniel glanced at it and agreed. Certainly no one at the Institute had ordered any.

"I don't suppose that the stock room in the Chemistry Department had any old stuff sitting around?" Brenda asked.

"I thought of that too and called them," Izzy said. "No dice. So, where do we go from here?"

Daniel sighed. "Carolyn is still top of my list as a suspect. I'm getting a search warrant for her house. We should go through Larramore's home study and see if anything suggests an alternate solution. I'd also like to check the coffee supply in her kitchen."

"What about the lover?" Brenda asked. "We need to find out who she's been seeing. I'm wondering if we should put a tail on her."

"I think that would be difficult," Daniel said. "If she's seeing someone at the Institute, they could be meeting in the Chemistry building. We can't have someone standing outside her office all day. It's hardly subtle."

"You're right. I think we might learn more by going through her phone records for the past six months. We should focus on the time period just prior to when she must have gotten pregnant," Brenda said. "I'll take care of it."

Daniel hated this part of a case, where he felt stymied and had to wait for a break. It was particularly galling because he had a hunch that Hannah could easily find out what he wanted to know. But there was no way he could ask for her help.

CHAPTER TWENTY-TWO

M Y PARENTS WERE SCHEDULED TO ARRIVE AT LAX AT noon, on Thanksgiving Day. The flight was on time, so I parked in the cell phone lot and waited for them to call me, after they collected their baggage. My mother was not the kind of woman who could possibly come to Los Angeles for a long weekend with just a carry-on.

After their call, I negotiated the hideous airport traffic and spotted them, waiting at the curb. Dad was wearing khaki pants and a white polo shirt, holding on to two large suitcases.

Mom was resplendent in a lime green dress, a white cardigan, and a white sunhat. During her days as a high school English teacher, she had always worn conservative clothes, but her retirement in Miami had brought out her true taste for bright colors. She had her hands full with shopping bags, stuffed with gift-wrapped presents. My parents had a habit of spoiling Zoe, showering her with gifts every year, whenever they saw her, and sending them by UPS in-between.

I pulled the car up, opened the trunk, and got out to give them both a hug.

"How was your flight?" I asked.

Mom made a face. "The guy sitting next to me had body odor. I've never been so glad to land."

"Are you hungry?" I asked. It was about dinnertime in Miami.

"You know me, honey," Dad said. "I could always have a little something to eat."

I resumed the driver's seat and pulled into the traffic. "Let's get you settled in your hotel and then we can go to the house. I planned on an early Thanksgiving dinner to allow for jet lag."

"I can't wait to finally meet your Daniel," Mom said. She was sitting next to me in the passenger seat, trying to get a good look at the ring on my left hand. I wasn't in a position to take it off the wheel and show it to her.

"He's looking forward to meeting you, too," I said. "He had to go into work this morning, but he's off for the rest of the holiday, so we should have a nice relaxing weekend."

At least, I hoped it would be relaxing. My stomach was in a knot and I wondered, not for the first time, why the prospect of introducing Daniel to my parents was making me feel like an insecure sixteen-year-old, instead of a competent, mature woman pushing forty.

CHAPTER TWENTY-THREE

D ANIEL WAS ANXIOUS TO FINALLY MEET HANNAH'S parents, but he hadn't had the luxury of a whole day off. In fact, the search warrant for the Larramore home had come through late the previous afternoon. He and Brenda had taken a team to the house at 7:00 a.m., when he was certain Carolyn would still be home.

"Here's what we're looking for," Daniel said. "We want his home computer, so we can go through his emails and papers. Search the study for financial records, and anything else suggesting a personal relationship with someone we may not yet be aware of. Try not to make too much of a mess. We're also searching the kitchen. I want to check out the coffee supply. Look everywhere for any small bottle with an unidentified substance, that might be our murder weapon."

Carolyn answered the doorbell, still in pajamas and a robe.

"What do you want now? Haven't we had enough conversations?"

"I'm afraid not, Dr. Larramore. I have a search warrant for your home. We need to examine your husband's study, among other things. We'll try not to disturb you."

Carolyn glared at him and opened the door. "It's hard enough dealing with the aftermath of a murdered husband, without half-a-dozen cops tramping around my house."

"Why don't you have a seat in the living room while we're searching, ma'am," Brenda said. "Officer Perez will stay with you."

She nodded to a young policewoman, who took Carolyn's arm and guided her to a comfortable chair. Carolyn sat, her hands in tight fists and her expression furious. Looking at her, Daniel almost felt guilty, until he reminded himself that she was his chief suspect.

He sent two of the evidence teams to start on the study and two others to search the master bedroom and all the bathrooms. He and Brenda began in the kitchen.

It was a spacious, modern and well-organized room. The cabinets were stocked with attractive dishes, silverware, and high-end cooking equipment. The pantry contained cans and other staples in labeled plastic containers. They searched it carefully, along with the spice drawers. Nothing suspicious. The coffee was in the freezer: one unopened bag of Peet's Espresso. Daniel put it in an evidence bag.

"Let's find out where they get their coffee," he said.

Carolyn was still in the living room, silent and angry. Daniel sat down opposite her.

"Dr. Larramore, where do you purchase your coffee?"

"Peet's on Westwood Boulevard," she said.

"Not the supermarket?" Brenda asked.

"The supermarket doesn't carry ground espresso."

"Did you and your husband both drink it?" Daniel asked.

Carolyn shook her head. "The espresso was for Edwin. I used to drink the Arabian Mocha Java, but since I got pregnant, I've been confining myself to herbal tea. One of many sacrifices I imagine mothers make for their children."

"I see," Daniel said. "Did Edwin purchase his own coffee?"

"Edwin delegated banal jobs like shopping to lesser mortals," Carolyn said. "It was my job to make sure we always had back-up coffee available for his office. He usually went through one bag a month."

"And how long ago did you purchase this bag?" Brenda asked.

She shrugged. "I don't remember. Probably over a month ago. I get them, two at a time, so we never run out."

"And do you always keep your extra coffee in the freezer?" Brenda asked.

"It stays fresher that way."

"Thank you, Dr. Larramore." Brenda said. "We should be finished soon. We're sorry to have troubled you."

The team in the study appeared with Edwin's computer and several file boxes full of papers.

Carolyn rose and walked toward them. "What are you taking?" she demanded.

"Those are financial records, ma'am." Brenda said.

Carolyn turned to Daniel. "Did it ever occur to you that I might need Edwin's financial records for my tax return?"

"Of course, Doctor," Daniel said. "I'll give you a receipt for what we've taken, and we will return everything that proves to be irrelevant to the investigation as soon as possible."

She glared at him as the team left the house. The two

who were checking out the bedroom and bathrooms reap-peared, with a small plastic bag. It seemed to contain the contents of the medicine cabinet: Tylenol, Mylanta, contact lens solution, cough syrup and cold medication. All those bottles probably contained nothing more than what was on the labels, but all the contents would need to be tested.

"Are we done?" Daniel asked.

They nodded.

"So, thanks to you, I have to go to the drug store and replace all of that," Carolyn said.

"I'm afraid so," Daniel said.

"I don't suppose you'd like to tell me what the hell you're looking for," Carolyn asked.

"Sorry, Dr. Larramore. You know we can't discuss it," Daniel answered.

As they left the house, Brenda said. "I just had a thought."

"Which was?"

"We've been assuming that the poison was added to the bottom of the coffee bag on Friday, or early Saturday morn-ing. What if Carolyn, or an accomplice, simply took a bag from the freezer, emptied it into another container, mixed a small amount with poison, replaced it on the bottom of the bag, and filled the bag with uncontaminated coffee?"

"I see," Daniel said. "Larramore would have finished most of the bag without any symptoms, until he got to the bottom."

"Right," Brenda said. "Unlike coffee bags from the super-market, which are vacuum packed and sealed tight, the ones you buy at Peet's or Starbucks aren't. They can easily be opened and closed again, without anyone noticing that the bag has been tampered with. If I'm right, alibis for the day before the murder, and the morning of, would be irrelevant."

"If you're right, then the only viable suspects would be those with access to the Larramore's home freezer. I wonder if the lab has identified the fingerprint on the coffee bag that didn't belong to him," Daniel said.

"If it belongs to Carolyn, unfortunately, that would tell us nothing. She's already said she purchased, and therefore handled, the coffee," Brenda said. "But, I'll call and see what they have."

"Thanks, Brenda. I'll head back to the station and have a quick look at what we've confiscated. I'm hoping to get home at a reasonable hour. My future in-laws are arriving this afternoon. Why don't you take off now and enjoy the rest of your Thanksgiving?"

CHAPTER TWENTY-FOUR

"Grandma!" Zoe ran for the front door and enveloped my mother's legs in a hug.

"Hello, Sweet Pea," Mom said, dropping her packages and leaning down to kiss her.

"How about me?" my father said.

Zoe grinned and held out her arms to be picked up. "Hi, Grandpa."

I guided them into the den, took drink orders, and brought in a tray with cheese, crackers and grapes. Emilia was off for the holiday weekend, so I was on my own for Thanksgiving dinner. Fortunately, she had cooked all the side dishes yesterday, so all I had to do was warm them up and put the turkey breast in the oven. I thought I could manage that and time everything so we could eat by five o'clock. I waited for the oven to reach 450, popped in the turkey, and took out the sweet potatoes, parsnip and apple puree and green beans.

"I have some presents for you, sweetheart," Mom said, opening her shopping bags. "Why don't you open this one first?"

Zoe ripped off the gift-wrap paper and held up a Princess Barbie.

"Thank you, Grandma."

My child was always polite. She had quite a collection of Barbies by now. They seemed to show up at every birthday party. They were neatly stored in one of her cabinets, and I had never seen her actually play with one. After the first Barbie, I took the precaution of saving the boxes for re-gifting or donation.

"Here's another one," my mother said, handing her the second box. Zoe opened it.

"Look Mommy, it's a Doctor Barbie."

Doctor Barbie was wearing scrubs and a white coat.

"Maybe she can deliver a baby for Princess Barbie." She proceeded to pull up the princess's ball gown and spread her legs.

I should never have allowed her to watch that Nova series on childbirth.

"I don't think Princess Barbie is pregnant, honey," I said. "Why don't you see what else Grandma brought for you?"

Grandma was eyeing me with disapproval. The mechanics of childbirth had never been discussed during my childhood.

"Here, Zoe. This one is from Grandpa," my father said.

Dad had taken the precaution of actually asking me for a suggestion. It was a set of Legos.

"These are great, Grandpa." Zoe's smile this time was genuine. "Can we play with it after dinner?"

"Absolutely," he said, looking quite pleased with himself.

"One more," Grandma said. "I thought you should have something special to wear for Thanksgiving dinner."

Zoe opened it, revealing a pink dress with sequins. She gave me her *you know I hate pink* look and I shrugged in sympathy. Ever since she had developed a preference in clothes, she would only wear black, white, navy and khaki.

"Way too risky to wear that," I said. "She'll get cranberry sauce all over it. We should save it for a special, non-food occasion."

Maybe I could exchange it later for something she might actually wear.

Just then, Daniel walked through the front door.

"Hi honey," I said. "Come meet my parents."

Daniel was looking very hot, and I could tell my mother was admiring his good looks and his very professional clothes. I knew he'd taken special care getting dressed this morning.

Daniel smiled, and held out his hand to shake my father's. "I've been looking forward to meeting both of you, Mr. and Mrs. Kramer."

"Oh, please," said my mother. "Esther and Max. We're practically family." She stood up and kissed him on the cheek. "I can't wait to learn all about you."

I escaped to the kitchen to lower the oven temperature, put in the vegetables to warm, and set the timer for thirty more minutes, leaving Daniel in my mother's clutches. After all, he was a tough cop and experienced in handling interrogations.

The dining room was already set with my good china. Ben, being an architect, had a weakness for beautiful things, and had insisted we pick out the accoutrements for formal dining when we got married. His parents had given us the Limoges china, and his grandmother had contributed her sterling silver. It looked very elegant, but he and I hadn't thrown very many fancy dinner parties during my residency. And I hadn't used the china since his death. Somehow, today seemed like the perfect occasion to demonstrate that I was a grown-up, with my own household.

I took out a bottle of Pinot Noir to go with dinner. Then I ventured back to the den. I heard laughter as I entered the room, and was relieved to see that Daniel was being his charming, amusing self. Mother seemed enchanted. I wondered how far she had gotten in her job interview for future son-in-law.

"Daniel was just telling me about his college days at Stanford," my mother said.

Good move, I thought. Like with most Jewish parents, education was valued above all, and Stanford was a credential only slightly less impressive than Harvard.

"So, Daniel, why would a Stanford lawyer choose to become a detective instead?" my mother asked, with her usual tact.

Clearly, Daniel hadn't mentioned that he'd actually dropped out of law school, because he'd hated it.

"Truthfully, Esther, because it's so much more interesting. Solving a crime requires putting together all the pieces of a complex puzzle. You need to understand the science of forensics, the psychology of motive, and the computer technology of tracing a suspect. When you have a complicated crime, it's immensely satisfying when you can solve it and achieve some justice. Corporate law is mostly about rich guys, arguing with other rich guys about money, or crafting deals that will make them even richer. Lawyers make more money than detectives, but at the end of the day, I don't think they make a real difference in people's lives. I guess I wanted to make a difference," Daniel said.

Mom was actually speechless, and I was impressed. I'd never heard Daniel articulate his love for his work in quite this way. He must have been rehearsing in advance of my parents' visit.

"Well," said Dad. "We're happy to be acquiring a detective into the family talent pool. I understand you two haven't set a date yet."

"No, we haven't," I said. "We need to get a house first, and settle in. There's no rush about the wedding. It's going to be small and intimate. We've both been married before."

"Rabbi's calendars get filled up quickly, so you'll need to plan in advance," Mom said.

I took a deep breath. "We aren't planning on a religious wedding, Mom. Daniel isn't Jewish, and neither one of us is observant. When the time comes, we'll find a judge, or ask a close friend to do the honors."

For a moment, my mother was silent. Just a moment.

"Are your parents okay with those plans?" Mom asked, turning to Daniel.

"They haven't asked, and I haven't discussed it with them. I don't imagine that they're fantasizing about three-hundred people at the country club. If they are, we'll let them down gently. At our age, it's about the marriage, not the wedding."

"Don't I get to be the flower girl, Mommy?" Zoe asked.

I put my arm around her and hugged. "I wasn't planning on a flower girl, sweetheart, but if you like, you can be my maid of honor."

At that point, I was saved by the bell, and I announced that dinner was ready. Everyone took their seats in the dining room, and I passed out wine, water and the first course salad. Conversation gave way to chewing. My father carved the turkey breast, and I served it with all the traditional side dishes.

"So, Hannah, I see you finally learned how to cook," my mother said.

Daniel was tactful enough not to disillusion her. After dinner, I brought the pie out and served it with vanilla bean ice cream.

"Emilia and I baked the pumpkin pie, Grandma," Zoe said.

After dinner, Zoe followed my father and Daniel into the den to try out her new Legos. My mother helped me clear the table and offered to help wash the dishes, which, being Limoges, couldn't go in the dishwasher. When she closed the kitchen door, so our conversation wouldn't be overheard, I knew I was in for it.

"So, Hannah, why didn't you tell me Daniel wasn't Jewish? What are you thinking? Are you planning to raise Zoe as a nothing?"

"I'm planning to raise her exactly as I was raised, in a secular household. Why does it matter to you? You never go to synagogue. Are you afraid Daniel's going to stage a pogrom in our living room?"

"We didn't have to go to synagogue. We lived in Brooklyn. Everyone was Jewish. How is she going to know who she is?"

"She's pretty smart, Mom. She'll figure it out."

My mother put the last of the dinner plates into the dish drainer, while I dried.

"If you ask me, she's too smart for her own good. She's only six. Why did you teach her about childbirth?"

"She asked, and it's what I do for a living," I said, trying hard to keep my temper. I knew, from experience, that the escalation of yelling would follow.

"I suppose you told her all about how the baby gets in as well as how it gets out."

I couldn't help it. I started to laugh. "She hasn't asked yet. When she does, I will tell her and I'll be as matter-of-fact about it as possible. I won't follow in your footsteps. You were so coy about it, I didn't have a clue, until I started reading romances in high school."

Mother picked up a towel to dry the pots. She was obviously thinking of a comeback.

"What kind of an example do you think you're setting for your child, living with a man, when you aren't married?"

I took a deep breath and let it out. "Mom, it's the twenty-first century. Everyone lives together first. I wish you'd stop talking to me as if I'm sixteen, and remember that I'm all grown up and capable of making my own decisions. I'm marrying a smart, kind, loving guy who's crazy about me and adores Zoe. Why don't you just try to get to know him?"

Mother finished drying the pots, and put them carefully back in the pot drawer. She folded the dishtowel and faced me.

"I admit he's very handsome and charming, but don't think that will change my opinions."

I hadn't thought it would. It was clearly going to be a very long weekend.

CHAPTER TWENTY-FIVE

B RENDA KNEW BETTER THAN TO EXPECT THAT SHE could
acquire any useful information over a holiday weekend, even if the lab had already done the fingerprint work
on the coffee bag. Certainly, the phone records she had
requested wouldn't be available until much later. None-
theless, she informed her parents that she was working on a
very high profile case and needed to head back to LA on
Friday.

Friday morning, she threw her bag in the trunk of her
car, and hugged her parents goodbye.

"I'm so sorry you can't stay for the whole weekend," her
mother said. "I was looking forward to having you come to
church with us on Sunday."

Avoiding that prospect, was one of the reasons Brenda
wanted to leave early. "I'm sorry too, Mom, but you know
how it is when you're a cop."

It had been a pleasant enough Thanksgiving dinner.
The meal was sumptuous and Brenda had enjoyed trading
cop stories with her father and two older brothers, all of
whom were in law enforcement. She could have done

without her mother's misguided effort to fix her up with one of her brother's colleagues, who had clearly been invited to dinner for just that reason.

Brenda pulled her car out of the driveway and headed for the 10 Freeway. Shortly before the entrance, she pulled over and took out her cell phone. She didn't like to make calls when she was driving, and she wanted to phone the lab. That way, she wouldn't have totally lied to her parents. She was working.

"Any chance you guys completed the fingerprint analysis of the coffee bag in the Larramore case?" she asked.

They had. The bag had Larramore's prints on it and one other partial print, but it was still unidentified.

"We ran it against every single print we collected from the entire Physics and Astronomy Department, along with his wife's. No match. No match in any Federal database either," the tech told her.

That was odd. Why weren't Carolyn's prints on the bag? Brenda had expected them to be there. Is it possible she put on latex gloves and wiped the bag clean before putting in the poison? Could the unidentified print belong to a lover? Clearly, this was going to be a topic of discussion at Monday's team meeting.

With a shrug, Brenda restarted her car and headed east toward Palm Springs, where Marcy was waiting for her. It was going to be their first romantic weekend alone and Brenda couldn't wait.

Her visit home had reminded her, however, that one day soon, she was going to have to come out to her Evangelical parents, and she was dreading the prospect. She hadn't even come out to Daniel, although she had a hunch that he suspected. Especially after he saw them together at the restaurant.

Oh well, she wasn't worried about her partner. She just didn't want her private life to become a topic in the male cops' locker room.

Daniel was in a cheerful mood when he reached the station on Monday morning. He didn't often get a four-day weekend, and he'd really liked Hannah's parents, although he sensed some underlying tension.

"So, did I pass?" he'd asked her that morning.

"It's not an exam," she said.

"I had a feeling your mother isn't thrilled that I'm not Jewish. Is that going to be a problem?"

"Are your parents concerned that I'm not Episcopalian?" she countered.

"They haven't asked," Daniel said. "They assume everyone's Episcopalian."

"Really? You mean they thought Hannah Kline was a WASP name?"

"Maybe they were too busy hosting their fiftieth anniversary party to notice," Daniel said.

Hannah laughed and deposited a kiss on the back of his neck.

"Let's not worry about it," she said. "Fortunately, we don't live in the world of arranged marriages."

"That's true," he said. "But when you marry someone, you also marry their family. I'd like to think that everyone is happy for us."

"My parents can be difficult," Hannah said, "but I am not prepared to let them drive a wedge between us."

The team settled down to a strategy session. Brenda presented the fingerprint information, as well as her hypothesis that the coffee could have been doctored at the Larramore home.

Izzy had worked over the weekend, and had tackled the financial records and emails.

"Boring," he said. "This guy was a professor, not a financier. He had a nice, institute pension plan with a little over half-a-million in it, and a brokerage account at UBS, amounting to a few hundred thousand. There was a joint checking account, and a small savings account. No Swiss banks or accounts hidden in the Cayman Islands. No suspicious large money transfers. No checks made out to recipients I couldn't easily identify. Whatever the motive was, I don't think it had anything to do with fraud or blackmail."

"What about his emails?" Daniel asked. "Anything grab you there?"

Izzy shook his head. "They all seemed mostly work-related. I kept looking for something that might have been sent to a friend or family member, but there was nothing. I finally investigated his family status. Only child, both parents deceased. The guy didn't seem to have any kind of social life."

"No hint of a mistress or other sexual relationship?" Brenda asked.

"If he was screwing someone, he was very careful not to send her any emails or texts. I did check to see if he had deleted anything interesting, but no luck."

"What about his will?" Daniel asked. "We need to get hold of his lawyer and find out what was in it."

"I can do that," Izzy said. "His wife was the beneficiary of his pension plan, and the house is community property. The brokerage account is in his name, so he could have left it to someone else. It's also possible that he owns property we don't know about. I'll find out."

Daniel sighed. "Everywhere we turn seems to be a dead end, except for the wife. We need to get their phone records as soon as possible, see if we can identify the lover, and think about how to find that chemical. The fact that her fingerprints aren't on the coffee is really suspicious to me. Perhaps it was her first mistake."

"Unless her lover purchased the coffee, eliminated his fingerprints, and put it in the freezer, or in Larramore's office," Brenda suggested.

"Also a possibility. The sooner we find this guy, the better."

"I don't suppose," Brenda said to Daniel, after the team had dispersed, "that Carolyn's obstetrician might know his identity."

"I doubt it," Daniel said. "And she wouldn't tell me if she knew."

CHAPTER TWENTY-SIX

I GOT TO MY OFFICE A LITTLE LATE ON MONDAY morning, after dropping my parents off at LAX for their flight. My mother had kissed my cheek, thanked me for a lovely weekend, and avoided saying anything about a wedding.

I suspected this was because she was hoping I'd come to my senses and change my mind.

Dad had been a little more forthcoming. "I like your guy, Hannah. But make sure you know what the complications could be, before you make it official."

I gave him a hug. "Not to worry. I'm all grown up now."

I hadn't scheduled any surgeries for this morning, so my only task for the day was to pay the office bills, my least favorite job. When I reached my desk, there was a phone message from Jackie, my realtor. I called her back.

I'd been debating over how to handle her, ever since I'd learned that she was Carolyn's mother. The whole situation was awkward. But, I liked Jackie and she really knew her Westside real estate. The solution I had reached was to suggest that we hold off looking until after the first of the year. Very few people listed their homes between Thanksgiving and New Year's, and that would give Daniel plenty of time to solve the murder.

"Jackie, how are you," I said. "I didn't get a chance to tell you how sorry I am about your son-in-law. I imagine you'll need to spend most of your time helping Carolyn."

"Carolyn is holding up," Jackie said. "I just wish the investigation was over, so she could move on. By the way, she just loves you. I wanted to thank you for being so supportive to her."

"She's been my patient for a long time, and I'm very fond of her," I said. "I'll do anything I can to help her. I was thinking we could hold off house hunting until after the New Year. I'm sure you'd like to spend as much time as possible, right now, with your daughter."

"That's very kind of you," Jackie said. "However, there is one house I'd like to show you this weekend, if you can make the time. I saw it Friday at a broker's open, and I think it meets all your criteria. If it's not right, then we can certainly take a break."

"OK, I said. "If you give me the information, I can meet you Saturday afternoon."

Jackie gave me the address and I wrote it down, checking it out online. On the computer, it looked like something we would like. Wouldn't it be nice if it was a home that actually worked for us?

CHAPTER TWENTY-SEVEN

D ANIEL WAS ENSCONCED IN A COMFORTABLE CHAIR IN the den, watching CNN, when Hannah arrived home.

"I got a call today from Jackie, our realtor," Hannah said, as she removed her coat.

Daniel muted the television and turned toward her. "What did she say?"

"There's a house she'd like me to look at on Saturday. I was planning to put house hunting on hold until after New Year's. By that time, I'm hoping Edwin Larramore's murder will be solved. At the moment, I'm feeling uncomfortable with the idea that Jackie might find out my fiancé is in charge of the investigation."

Daniel was feeling uncomfortable as well. It was never a good thing when a personal relationship crossed the boundaries of a murder case. But he wasn't sure he shared Hannah's confidence in his abilities.

"I wish I could promise you it'll be solved by then. We're a bit stuck. I also wish I could discuss it with you. I miss your insights, Miss Marple."

Hannah came over to where he was sitting, and gave him

a hug. "I wish I could help, but...patient confidentiality. For the record, in case you have Carolyn on your suspect list, I don't believe for a moment that she would be capable of killing anyone."

Daniel shrugged. Obviously, she had no idea that Carolyn was his number one candidate for the murderer.

"Anyone is capable of killing with the right provocation. Couldn't you kill someone, if he was threatening Zoe's life?"

"I don't know, Daniel, but I sure as hell would do whatever I could to disable him. On another more cheerful topic, just in case this house turns out to be a real find, can you and Zoe come over to see it?"

"I think that's a bad idea, Hannah. I don't think I should meet Jackie or have anything to do with her right now. What if she turns out to be a witness?"

"What if I fall madly in love with this house?"

"Why don't we cross that bridge if we come to it?" Daniel said.

CHAPTER TWENTY-EIGHT

BRENDA WAS ON A ROLL THE NEXT MORNING. THE telephone data had finally come through for both Edwin and Carolyn Larramore. Izzy had run it though a computer program that identified all the phone numbers, and organized them by frequency. He was sorting through Edwin's calls, and Brenda was working on Carolyn's. It didn't take long to find what she was looking for.

"Why are you grinning like a Cheshire Cat?" Daniel asked, as he walked in and dropped his briefcase on his desk.

Brenda rotated her computer monitor to face him.

"Oliver Wilson," she said. "There are four months worth of regular calls between Carolyn's mobile and his. They stop around the middle of July. I'll bet you lunch that she was having an affair with that hot Australian. Why else would she be talking regularly with a member of her husband's research group?"

Daniel gave her a high five. "Thank goodness. Now we have something to do. I was beginning to think we'd never get a break in this case. Too bad that fingerprint on the coffee bag wasn't a match for his. We'd have a new prime suspect."

"You can't have everything," Brenda said. "Why don't we go interview him again?"

~

Oliver Wilson was busy at his computer terminal when Daniel and Brenda knocked on his door.

"We need a few more minutes of your time, Professor," Daniel said.

Oliver shrugged and motioned the two of them to sit down.

"How well did you know Carolyn Larramore?" Daniel asked.

"Not very well. I met her at a department reception, and ran into her a few times when she stopped by to visit her husband. Why are you asking?"

"We were wondering why there were so many calls between your cell phone and hers, over a four month period. Were you having an affair, Professor?" Daniel said.

Oliver's mouth tightened. "We were friends," he said. "We shared the same habit of having morning coffees at the campus coffee shop, so we often had them together. She's a nice woman, smart, and interesting to talk to."

"I see," Brenda said. "You seem to have talked on the phone quite often. Why did you stop? After July, there were no more phone calls. Did you argue?"

"No," Oliver said. "Carolyn was concerned that Edwin might find out about our friendship and be angry. She said he could be very vindictive and could even sabotage my career. She thought we should stop phoning and having coffee together, so we did."

"Did you know she was pregnant?" Daniel asked.

"Not until I saw her at Edwin's memorial service. She never said."

"Here's our problem, Dr. Wilson," Daniel said. "We're trying to figure out how Carolyn Larramore got pregnant. Her husband had a vasectomy. She became pregnant during the time you and she were 'having coffee' together. I'm asking you again, were you her lover? Is there a possibility that you're the father of her child?"

Oliver's face blanched. "We only made love once," he said.

"Once is enough for conception," Brenda commented.

"Why didn't she tell me?" Oliver asked.

"What would you have done about it?" Daniel asked.

"I'd have asked her to leave the bastard and come back to Australia with me," Oliver said. "Look, Detectives, you want to know how I started having coffee with Carolyn?"

"Absolutely," Brenda said.

"I was walking down the hall past Edwin's office and I heard him yelling. A few minutes later, Carolyn came out, in tears, with a nasty bruise on her arm. I was waiting for the elevator, and I offered to buy her a cup of coffee. That's how it started."

Oliver paused and took a sip of water from a bottle on his desk.

"Everyone thinks Larramore walked on water, but he was nasty, controlling and abusive. He drove his students harder than anyone in the department, and didn't credit them for their work. He was shagging Suzanne, his newest student, who was stupid enough to worship him. Carolyn deserved to have a friend. God knows she needed one."

"How do you know he was sleeping with Suzanne?" Daniel asked.

"The whole group knew. She followed him around like a lovesick puppy and was constantly in his office. She didn't make any secret of her infatuation. I believe the way she put it, was that she was *dating* him. I think the poor girl had the fantasy that he might leave his wife for her."

"Do you think he would have?" Brenda asked.

"Please!" Oliver said. "Do you have any idea how often married professors fool around with students? She was a play thing. He'd have gotten bored and dropped her, as soon as the next sexy student came along. The guy was a cold fish."

"Were you ever at the Larramore home when he wasn't there?" Brenda asked.

"The only time I ever set foot in Larramore's house was after the memorial."

"What about Larramore's office? Were you ever in there when he wasn't?"

"Why would I be? Any data I needed was accessible on my own computer."

"Well, thank you, Professor. You've been very helpful," Brenda said, as they left his office.

"I guess I owe you a lunch," Daniel said. "Good work."

"I don't think Oliver was faking when he found out he could be the father. It's hard to make your face turn white like that," Brenda said.

"Well, that information certainly provides an additional reason for Carolyn to kill her husband, or a possible motive for Suzanne to kill her lover. What if he had broken up with her? She would have been humiliated and furious, not to mention in need of an alternate thesis advisor," Daniel said.

"But where would either of them get the arsenic compound?" Brenda asked. "That's the missing link. We've got motive and opportunity, but until we can connect it to the means, we don't have a case."

"That does seem to be the sticking point," Daniel agreed.

"Let's worry about it tomorrow," Brenda said. "I think you should take me to Nate 'n Al's in Beverly Hills. I have a yen for deli."

CHAPTER TWENTY-NINE

T HE NEXT DAY WAS SATURDAY. I INVITED ZOE TO COME and make rounds with me in the morning, but she turned me down. Apparently, she thought playing Legos with Daniel was much more fun than watching Mommy take surgical staples out of incisions. I was beginning to despair of her future career in medicine.

At one o'clock, I met Jackie at the house. It was a one story, mid-century modern, on a quiet cul-de-sac, in the foothills north of Sunset. From the street, it was nothing special. A dark wood door, white stucco, and narrow horizontal windows that provided privacy from the street. There were a few large shade trees, and a modest garden. When Jackie opened the door, I caught my breath. From the entry way, you could see through to the back of the house, where a wall of floor to ceiling windows provided a spectacular view of the hills and adjacent canyon. The living room was spacious and flowed into the dining area.

"What do you think?" Jackie asked.

"Love the view," I said, as I walked into the kitchen.

The kitchen was still stuck in the sixties, with gold appliances, avocado green linoleum and Formica countertops. Most of it would have to be gutted and replaced, but the cabinetry was solid teak and beautiful, and the workflow was right.

A wing to the left contained a spacious master bedroom and bath, and an adjoining study, lined with built-in bookshelves and two desks. To the right, were three smaller rooms. Zoe could have her own bedroom and playroom, to be converted into a study when she was older. We could even have a guest room. The bedroom wings were carpeted in orange shag, but I could deal with that.

"The original owners built this house in the sixties, and just died recently. Their heirs are anxious to sell, and it's very well priced, because most couples want something more traditional and two stories," Jackie said.

I walked slowly along the windows, and through the glass door onto a large deck with a hot tub. There was a small, grassy back yard, fenced with clear Lucite. I took a deep breath and took in the view.

"It's got great bones," I said. "I was married to an architect. He taught me how to look at a house. Assuming that this one doesn't have a small fortune's worth of deferred maintenance, it could be perfect."

"Are you divorced?" Jackie asked.

I shook my head. "My husband passed away before Zoe was born. That's how I understand something of what Carolyn must be going through."

"Did you have a good marriage?" Jackie asked.

I nodded. "Ben was a lovely man."

"Edwin, my son-in-law, wasn't. Frankly, I think she's better off without him. He was a controlling, self-centered, son-of-a-bitch."

"I'm sorry to hear that. Raising a child alone is a challenge."

"She's got a good role model," Jackie said. "Her father left us for his secretary when Carolyn was four. The only good thing I can say about him is that he was a big real estate developer. I learned real estate from him, in addition to getting a substantial chunk of child support. I hadn't planned to spend my life selling houses, but real estate has been good to me."

"What did you want to do?" I asked.

"Believe it or not, I wanted a career in academia. Unfortunately, I was the wrong sex at the wrong time. I never could find the kind of job I wanted. I'm proud of my daughter. She's succeeded where I failed. Without the burden of a dominating husband, I think she'll blossom, professionally."

"I hope so," I said. "There are few things as satisfying as having a career you love. If it's okay, I'd like to take some photos and then go home and discuss it with my fiancé. I'm considering making an offer."

"Okay, you guys. We need to have a family conference," I said. "I just fell in love with a house."

I retrieved some ice cream from the freezer and dished it out at the kitchen table. Then, I turned on my phone and took them through the many detailed pictures.

"What do you think?"

"I don't like the orange carpet, Mommy," Zoe said.

"Me neither. We can replace it. Do you like the bedroom with the little garden outside, and the playroom next to it?"

"Can I pick out the colors for my rooms?" she asked.

"I'll take that as a yes," I said.

She nodded. "I'm done with my ice cream. Can I go and play?"

"Sure," I said, noticing that she had left half a bowl of mint chocolate chip ice cream.

I marveled at her ability to stop eating when she was full. No wonder she was so thin. Maybe I could learn how to do it. I resisted the temptation to finish off her leftovers.

"What do you think, Daniel?"

"I love the view, the hot tub and the study," he said

"But you're hesitating. What don't you like?"

Daniel sighed. "It's Jackie. She's the mother-in-law of the victim and a potential witness. I've avoided meeting her, but if I do business with her, it could compromise the investigation. It's just not ethical. I'm sorry, Hannah. I almost wish you hadn't gone to see the house."

"It certainly turned out to be an aggravating exercise in avoidance. I had to lie to Jackie about why my fiancé couldn't come right way to view it," I sighed, and took one last, lingering look at the photos. "I suppose we can always find another house when the case is solved. And, if necessary, a different realtor."

Daniel stood up and came over to my side of the table. I rose to join him and he put his arms tightly around me. I leaned against his chest and he kissed my forehead.

"Thanks love," he said. "I knew you'd understand."

I did understand, but it didn't keep me from feeling really frustrated.

CHAPTER THIRTY

IT WAS MONDAY MORNING, AND DANIEL WAS BUSY connecting his computer to the LCD projector in the department conference room.

At the beginning of the case, the room had been populated by a dozen detectives and patrolmen, who had been assigned to help with the canvassing and interviews that were so time-consuming during the first week of investigation. As time had gone by without a solution, detectives had been pulled off and reassigned to other cases, and the team had dwindled down to Daniel, Brenda and Izzy.

Daniel pulled a projection screen down, covering the whiteboard with all its photos and notes.

"What are you up to Boss?" Izzy asked.

"Don't laugh," Daniel said. "I made a spreadsheet."

Izzy suppressed a chortle. "A spreadsheet of what? You've never used a database program before."

"There's always a first time," Daniel said. "I thought I'd bring us into the twenty-first century and organize all the information. The rows contain every suspect we know, who had contact with the victim. The columns are motive, means and opportunity."

Brenda glanced at the projection. "Everyone seems to have a motive and there's lots of opportunity. The means are the real problem."

"Agreed," Daniel said. "Let's review these together, and see if anyone can come up with an angle we haven't thought of. You both know most of what's here, so let's focus on the new information. We know Larramore was abusive. That's been verified by two independent sources, his ex-wife, and his current wife's lover, whom we recently identified as Oliver Wilson. Carolyn was pregnant and unhappily married. She also had opportunity."

Brenda chimed in. "We know that Carolyn purchased all of Edwin Larramore's coffee, which leaves us with an interesting point to be explained. Her fingerprints should have been on the bag we retrieved from his office, but they weren't. This suggests that the killer wiped it clean to remove all prints."

Daniel continued. "Carolyn is a chemist with the skill, knowledge and equipment to synthesize the poison. Although, why she would have used such an obscure chemical is a mystery. Unfortunately, we have no evidence she ever purchased the precursor chemicals."

"Next on the list is Suzanne Baron," Brenda said. "Daniel and I need to re-interview her today, in light of recent information. Oliver Wilson told us it was common knowledge in the group that she was having an affair with Larramore. Perhaps he dumped her. That would provide a motive."

"I have some new information from the video guys," Izzy said. "They were able to positively identify Suzanne Baron, entering the building at 4:45 p.m. on Friday, shortly after

Larramore himself. Suzanne left shortly before Larramore did."

"Thanks," Daniel said. "That's very helpful. Let's move on. Oliver Wilson also informed us that Carolyn ended their affair, because she was concerned Larramore would sabotage his career if he found out. When Carolyn became pregnant, Larramore must have realized his wife had a lover, because he'd had a vasectomy. What if he learned that the lover was Oliver and threatened him? That could certainly motivate a murder. Once again, there's opportunity and motive, but no clear access to means."

"His two other graduate students also had clear motives," Brenda went on. "We discussed that earlier, and there's no new information. There's nothing new on the ex-wife either. She was in town, but they'd been divorced for twenty years, and we have no indication she ever entered the Physics building."

"I've added one more person to the list. Her name is Jackie Cantor. During the memorial reception, Hannah found out that Jackie is Carolyn's mother. Unfortunately, she's also our realtor. We've had to stop house hunting until we solve the case."

"Have you interviewed her yet?" Izzy asked.

Daniel shook his head. "I'm hoping Brenda can do that. I'm laying low. Hannah mentioned that Jackie really disliked her son-in-law and felt he had impeded Carolyn's career. She also had access to the Larramore kitchen. She's not a serious suspect, but she might be able to provide some useful information."

"I'll track her down today, boss," Brenda said.

"I'm going to focus on the poison," Daniel said. "We've been drawing a blank so far. I'm going to call Professor McKenzie again, ask what happened to the original stuff that was synthesized at UC San Diego. Izzy, can you do a background check on all the faculty in the Physics, Astronomy and Chemistry departments, and see if there are any connections to the UCSD Chemistry department?"

Izzy nodded.

Daniel took a final sip of his coffee. "Come on," he said to Brenda. "Let's see if we can find Suzanne."

Suzanne was in her office, dressed in black jeans and a black turtleneck, her face pale without makeup. Daniel thought her long blonde hair looked as if it needed a wash. A few open textbooks were set out on her desk.

She looked up in surprise when Daniel and Brenda knocked at her office door and entered. "Detectives, what is it?"

Daniel seated himself.

Brenda leaned against the door.

"We need to ask you a few questions. You haven't been entirely truthful with us. You told us you went directly home after the conference. But the security video shows you entering the Physics building at 4:45 p.m. on Friday," he said.

She shrugged. "I must have forgotten. I probably just ran to my office for a few minutes, to pick up a book or some papers."

"You were there for an hour and a half," Brenda said. "You arrived shortly after Dr. Larramore did, and left just before he left. Did you meet with him? We were told the two of you were having an affair."

Suzanne's face fell. "I loved him. I certainly didn't kill him."

"Did he love you?" Daniel asked. "Or was he going to break up with you?"

"You've got it all wrong," she said. "Edwin said I was the most exciting woman he'd ever met. He was a very passionate, adventurous man, especially in the bedroom. His wife was very conventional, with no imagination. He'd strayed before, but we've been together since I came to the Institute."

"I see," Daniel said. "Tell me how you managed your affair. How did you see each other privately?"

"Edwin worked a lot at night. Some of those nights we went to hotels. He was very careful. We never went to the same hotel twice, and he always paid his bill in cash."

"Could you be a little more specific about what you mean by *adventurous*?" Brenda asked. She had her notebook out and was writing rapidly.

Suzanne smiled. "Edwin was into the BDSM world. He liked to tie me up, and he got turned on by spanking, but mostly, he loved inventing scenes. We'd make up scenarios and act them out."

"For example?" Daniel asked.

"There was one where he was a CIA agent and I was a spy, and he was interrogating me. We took turns making them up. He loved my imagination. I was very good at it."

"Did you like BDSM as well?" Brenda asked.

"If you haven't tried it, you won't understand," Suzanne said. "But the hint of danger, the lack of control, and the possibility of pain can be a tremendous turn-on. Edwin wasn't my first lover who was into it."

"Any other adventures?" Daniel asked. He wondered why, after all his years in the LAPD, he was still surprised when a woman who came across as smart, pretty and sweet turned out to like kinky sex. There was no accounting for taste.

"There was the Swingers Club. It wasn't for BDSM. It was mostly for people who liked threesomes and foursomes. A previous partner introduced him. You have to know someone to get in. No one uses his or her own name. We were Ted and Alice." She giggled.

"I'll need the address," Daniel said.

Suzanne glanced at him and then at Brenda. "They won't let you in," she said.

"That's our problem," Daniel said. "The address, please."

Suzanne pulled out her phone and wrote down the information. It was in Van Nuys.

"Another question," Brenda asked. "Did Larramore give you a key to his office?"

"No," she said. "Why would he? I only went there when he was in."

"Did he promise to leave his wife for you?" Brenda asked. "What did you think was going to happen with this affair?"

"We didn't discuss it," Suzanne said. "Anyway, I didn't want to marry him. He was twice my age. I wanted to finish my PhD, enjoy fabulous sex with an exciting, experienced man, and then get a job. I didn't want to be tied down, at least not that way, and I don't think he would have responded well to me nagging him to get a divorce. We understood one another."

"Were you with him Friday afternoon, after the conference?" Brenda asked.

Suzanne nodded. "We had a quickie on the sofa. He was in a really good mood after being the star lecturer. Then, I left. We were going to go to the club Saturday night."

"I see," Daniel said. "Well, thank you for being so forth-coming. We may have more questions later."

He rose and nodded to Brenda, who opened the door.

"Well, that was certainly eye opening," she said, as they waited for the elevator. "It brings up all sorts of new possibilities."

"Just what we need. More possibilities. We can't sort out the ones we have."

"You need some coffee," Brenda said.

They walked across campus to the nearest coffee shop. Brenda ordered a mocha without whipped cream and Daniel had black coffee. They split a blueberry scone.

"So," Daniel said. "Do you have a hot date Saturday night or would you like to stake out a swingers club with me?"

Brenda laughed. "How are you going to explain that one to Hannah?"

"I'll think of something."

"Actually, I do have a date Saturday night, but I can reschedule."

"Anyone special?" Daniel asked.

Brenda took a gulp of her mocha and looked at him. "You're a detective. You've probably already figured out I'm seeing Marcy."

"I suspected you were. But I wasn't sure. I was hoping you trusted me enough to tell me. We've worked together for three years now. I'd like it if you thought of me as your friend, not just your partner."

Brenda sighed. Daniel thought it sounded like a sigh of relief.

"I do trust you Daniel, but you know what the LAPD is like. The best way to keep a secret is to tell no one. My sex life is no one else's business."

"My lips are sealed," Daniel said. "Hannah figured it out as well, but she would never violate your privacy. Do your parents know?"

"Are you kidding? My mother would pray for me and try to get me to undergo conversion therapy. My father would probably kick me out of the family. If I ever get serious enough about someone to want to get married, I'll have to tell them, but I'm in no rush."

Daniel nodded. "Let's figure out what's next. Can you call on Jackie Cantor and see if she provides any interesting additional clues? I'm going to work on the arsenic."

"It should be interesting checking out the swingers club," Brenda said. "We can find out who owns the place. I wonder if Larramore met someone there he knew, who didn't want to be identified. That could provide a motive for murder."

Daniel nodded. "Unfortunately, we don't need any more motives. We need means."

The two of them returned to the station, where Brenda typed up her notes and made an appointment to meet with Jackie later that afternoon.

Daniel phoned Professor McKenzie. "Professor, just one more question. When someone finishes working with a chemical, what happens to it? I was wondering about the supply of Nickel Diarsine synthesized by your graduate student."

"Old chemicals get disposed of in a chemical hazard bin.

Sometimes the graduate student throws them out. Sometimes they just leave them and whoever takes over the space will get rid of them."

"Is it possible that a chemical could be overlooked and just sit in the lab for years?" Daniel asked.

"Not that lab," McKenzie said. "It was completely overhauled about twenty years ago with new hoods, sinks and cabinets. Chemicals are never allowed to be present in a construction zone."

"I see," Daniel said. "Thanks Professor."

That was a dead end. Daniel hoped Brenda would have more luck than he had.

CHAPTER THIRTY-ONE

BRENDA HAD SCHEDULED THE INTERVIEW WITH Carolyn's mother in her real estate office. She worked with a large firm in Brentwood and had a corner room, tastefully appointed with traditional furniture and comfortable client chairs.

Jackie herself was wearing a tailored gray suit with a pencil skirt, button-down white blouse, and sensible heels. Her ash blonde hair (a favorite dye color for older women who had turned gray) was fashionably cut and in perfect order. She wore chunky square gold earrings and a thick gold bracelet. Brenda assessed the jewelry as real, meaning Jackie probably sold a good many houses.

Jackie shook Brenda's hand, motioned her to sit, and asked how she could be of help.

"I'm one of the detectives investigating the death of your son-in-law. We've had some difficulty learning anything about him, beyond what Dr. Larramore's scientific colleagues and your daughter have to say."

"And you think I can give you information?"

Brenda took out her notebook and pen. "We haven't

been able to locate any friends or acquaintances outside of his work. I thought you might have a different point of view about his life and character."

Jackie sat back in her ergonomic office chair. "You haven't missed much, Detective. Edwin had no friends. He was quite antisocial. I, myself, rarely saw him. I got together with my daughter for dinner on nights he was working. There were no family events that I can describe to you. He had no family of his own left, and no interest in becoming part of ours."

"You sound as if you didn't like him very much," Brenda said.

"I didn't. I know one isn't supposed to speak ill of the dead, but Edwin was not a likable man."

"Why not?" Brenda asked.

Jackie glanced out the window, with its view of San Vicente Boulevard, as if she was weighing what she was going to say next. "He was very controlling, quite reserved and incapable of making polite conversation. I never wanted Carolyn to marry him. I thought it was a mistake from the beginning."

"Do you know why she did?"

Jackie ruefully shook her head. "I think she was besotted with the idea that this famous scientist was interested in her. She probably had fantasies about their sharing an academic life together. But he manipulated her into sacrificing her career for his."

"How so?" Brenda asked.

"My daughter is a brilliant and talented scientist. If she hadn't been married to him, she would have had her choice of prestigious academic jobs. Instead, she stayed at the Institute, in a dead-end position. I don't know if she can recover from that, professionally."

"Do you think she loved him?"

Jackie paused. "I think she did at the beginning, but he was so abusive. He always denigrated her, interrupted her, argued with her conclusions, and made her feel small."

"Do you know if he ever abused her physically?"

Jackie shook her head. "I don't know. She never said. But verbal abuse can be just as harmful. He didn't want her to have friends or a life outside of their marriage. I had the impression she didn't even tell him when she saw me."

"When was the last time you saw Edwin?"

"I don't remember, exactly. It was probably about two months ago. I had gone over to the house to bring Carolyn a book I'd bought for her, *What to Expect When You're Expecting*. We were drinking tea in the kitchen, when he came home earlier than usual. He seemed very annoyed to see me and was quite rude, so I left."

"How did he feel about Carolyn's pregnancy?" Brenda asked.

Jackie raised her eyebrows. "I had the impression that the last thing in the world he was interested in was becoming a father."

"How often do you see your daughter?"

"Since he died, I try to drop in at least twice a week to take her to dinner or keep her company. She's having a difficult time," Jackie said.

"What about when Edwin was alive? Did you go to their house often?" Brenda asked.

"Not often and never when he was home. Carolyn would call me if he was working late, or spending Saturday in the lab, and we would do something together, a movie or shopping. Sometimes we just stayed in the den and watched TV together."

"Did you notice any change in their relationship during the weeks prior to his death?" Brenda asked.

"I didn't see them together, Detective, but Carolyn seemed more depressed and withdrawn. I was worried about her."

"Is there anyone else you can think of who knew Edwin well, or who might have a different perspective?"

Jackie shook her head. "Sorry, Detective. I wish I could be more helpful."

"I appreciate your time," Brenda said. "I'll phone if I think of more questions."

"Anytime," Jackie said, rising and escorting Brenda to the door.

More of the same, Brenda thought, feeling frustrated that the interview hadn't yielded any new insight. It was too bad about medical confidentiality. She was willing to bet that Hannah had some useful information.

CHAPTER THIRTY-TWO

I WAS IN A BLUE MOOD AFTER THE WEEKEND. I'D REALLY been excited about that house, and hadn't enjoyed calling Jackie and telling her we weren't going to make an offer. I hated lying to anyone and this whole situation was making me squirm. I wanted to solve the damn murder myself so we could get on with our lives. This was difficult to do, as Daniel had shared no information. I wondered if I could change that.

I waited until came home, changed, and was sitting in his favorite chair with the margarita I'd made for him, to go along with the chicken chili Emilia had cooked for dinner.

As I perched myself on the well-upholstered chair arm, he asked, "So, how'd it go with the realtor?

"She wasn't happy when I told her we weren't making an offer."

"What excuse did you use?"

"Neither of us had the time and energy for the major upgrades the house required. That's not true, of course. I'd love to remodel that kitchen and I really liked the house."

Daniel put his drink aside and drew me onto his lap.

"I'm sorry sweetheart. It's a rotten coincidence that she's related to Larramore. You can't be any more frustrated than I am. This case is making me crazy."

"I know you haven't said anything about it because of Carolyn," I said. "But is there any part of it, unrelated to her, that you can talk about? Sometimes a fresh brain helps."

Daniel chewed on his lower lip, so I knew he was considering my suggestion. I kissed his forehead, and played with the hair on the back of his neck, while he thought about it.

"Here's what I can tell you about it. But it doesn't leave this room."

"Of course. I'll be the soul of discretion."

"Larramore was poisoned, in his coffee, with a rare chemical called Nickel Diarsine. The only reference to it is in a few papers from UC San Diego, published in the 70's."

"Where could the killer have gotten it?" I asked.

"That's the problem. It can't be bought and must be synthesized. Only one company sells the key precursor chemicals in the US. But we couldn't link any of their sales to any of our suspects."

"Was that chemical the reason we were able to have a weekend in La Jolla?"

Daniel nodded. "We went to San Diego so I could interview one of the two authors of the paper, a guy named McKenzie. He's 90 years old and long retired, but he remembered. The person who did the actual work was one of his graduate students, a woman named Jaycee Neuman."

"Have you located her?"

"No luck," Daniel said. "She seems to have dropped off the face of the earth. No subsequent publications, no driver's license, no death certificate, nothing in any Federal or State database. The choice of that chemical as the murder weapon makes no sense."

I ran my hands over Daniel's shoulders. I could tell he was tense. "Do you have any suspects, besides my patient, who might have been interested in murdering Larramore?"

"Larramore was a bastard. I've got loads of suspects, all with great motives and decent opportunity to poison him, but I can't link any of them to the diarsine."

"I see why you're tearing your hair out," I said. "Daniel, is it possible that Jaycee Neuman took the chemical with her when she left UCSD? Maybe she thought she'd do more research with it later on, and never did. Could she somehow be connected to one of your suspects?"

"That's an interesting idea, Hannah. You're thinking like a cop. We've been looking into whether anyone on our list has any connection to UCSD. Maybe we'll get a break that way."

"What's your next step?" I asked.

"I was going to tell you about that," he said. "You may not like it. I hope you didn't make any plans for us, for Saturday night. Brenda and I are going on a stakeout."

"Really, where?" I asked.

"It's a swinger's club in Van Nuys," Daniel said.

"You're going to a swinger's club?! Without me? Isn't that above and beyond the call of duty? "

"Relax. We're not participating. We're just going to sit in our car, eat junk food, photograph all the people who go in, and get their license plate numbers."

"I could come with you. Brenda could check out the license plates and we could go in there under cover."

"Very funny," Daniel said.

"I'm being serious. I always wanted to be Nancy Drew."

"Forget it."

"Jealous?"

"Maybe. You're one hot tamale, but you're my hot tamale."

"Seriously though, why are you interested in a swinger's club?"

"Edwin Larramore was a member," Daniel said. "We're wondering if he saw someone there who didn't want to be seen."

I reached over and took a long swallow of his Margarita. "Oh well, it would have been fun to go with you. I've always wanted to try dressing like a bimbo."

Daniel grinned. "Why don't we go upstairs and do an impromptu fashion show?"

CHAPTER THIRTY-THREE

THE AROMA OF KENTUCKY FRIED CHICKEN FILLED THE interior of Brenda's black Honda Civic, which was parked across the street from an ordinary looking, ranch-style tract house in Van Nuys. According to real estate records, the owners were Nate and Edna Fitch. Nate was also the owner of an auto repair place on Oxnard Street. Edna, when she wasn't hosting sex parties, worked at Costco.

In addition to the food supply, Daniel had come prepared with night vision goggles, a camera, and a small, department laptop. There were a number of cars scattered along the street, so while they weren't worried about being too conspicuous, they had parked as far as possible from the nearest street light.

Brenda reached into the bucket and handed Daniel a chicken thigh and a napkin. They'd ordered small Cokes. Bladders were always a problem on a stakeout.

They'd arrived shortly before 8:00 p.m., and most of the guests didn't appear until after 9:00 p.m. Six couples arrived, almost entirely older men with attractive young women.

Brenda used the goggles to read license plates, which Daniel wrote down. They tried to get photos of the couples as they entered the house, but it was hard in the dark, and they weren't sure if Photoshop could produce identifiable pictures.

"I wonder how many of those women are escorts," Brenda said.

"Probably a few. We can share the photos with the guys in Vice later, and see if they can identify anyone. I'm more interested in the men."

"Daniel, that man looks familiar. I could swear I've seen him before. I just can't place him."

The man in question was tall and stooped, with a halo of white hair.

"Let's see if we can pull up his plate," Daniel said.

They waited until the street quieted and it appeared that no other guests were joining the party. They didn't want the computer light to illuminate the interior of their car when Daniel accessed the police DMV database.

"Well, what do you know? The car belongs to George Taylor, Larramore's department chairman."

"No kidding," Brenda said. "I wonder who the woman is."

"Definitely not his wife."

"Do you suppose he encountered Larramore here, was afraid to be exposed, and killed him?" Brenda theorized.

"Certainly possible, although it would seem they were evenly matched. Both of them would have been at the same swingers club with women who weren't their wives. Which means Taylor could have exposed Larramore as well. We'll have to find out more about the dynamic between them."

"I suppose you're going to want to interview the Fitches tomorrow," Brenda said.

"I don't want to interfere with your weekend," Daniel said. "But I would like a look inside that house. If we wait for Monday, we'll have to talk to them at work."

"As long as I make it to my rescheduled dinner date tomorrow night, I'm with you," Brenda said. "I'd like a peek into the facilities myself."

It was well after midnight when Daniel got home. He tiptoed into the bedroom and undressed as quietly as possible, behind the closed bathroom door, so as not to disturb Hannah. He needn't have bothered. She was wide awake when he came to bed.

"So, did you have a foursome?" she asked.

"It was a total orgy," he answered, grinning.

"Really," she said, rolling over on top of him and pinning him beneath her. "Tell me all about it."

"Just one hot bimbo after another," he said. "But none of them was a redheaded surgeon, so I didn't bother."

"I told you, you should have taken me with you," she said. "I suppose you'd like a reward for your virtue."

"It would be nice," Daniel said.

It was.

CHAPTER THIRTY-FOUR

D ANIEL FIGURED THAT AFTER A NIGHT OF WILD SEX, THE Fitches would sleep in. So, he and Brenda arrived in Van Nuys at noon. They parked across the street and rang the bell. It was answered by a tall, stocky man, with five-o'clock shadow, and an almost bald head surrounded by a short, dark fringe of closely clipped hair. He was wearing a maroon terry bathrobe and leather slippers. Thick, dark chest hair peeked through the V of his robe.

"Yes?" he asked.

"Mr. Fitch?" Daniel showed his badge. "LAPD. We'd like a word with you and Mrs. Fitch."

"What for? We haven't done anything." Nate Fitch tried to close the door but Daniel's foot was in the way.

"I didn't say you'd done anything, but you may be a witness. If you don't want to talk to us here, we can drive you down to the station."

Fitch glared at Daniel, but released the door, allowing the two of them to enter.

"Who is that?" a woman's voice called.

"It's the police, Edna. They want to talk to us," Fitch said.

A woman emerged from the back of the house, holding a mug of coffee. She was tall and lanky, with a long, horsey face and thick, bleached blonde hair. She was wearing jeans, a cropped tank top, and long, dangling silver earrings.

"What about?" she asked.

"Why don't we all sit down, and I'll explain," Daniel said.

Nate motioned them into the living room. Daniel looked around. The room was furnished with two cheap leather sofas, a large wood coffee table, and a reclining chair. Evidence of last night's gathering was present with almost empty wine glasses, beer mugs, crushed napkins and a snack tray that still held the remnants of pretzels and peanuts. The Fitches seated themselves together on a sofa. Daniel and Brenda did the same, opposite them.

"We're aware you're running a swinger's club here," Daniel began.

"We're not doing anything illegal," Nate interrupted. "If we throw parties for our friends, what anyone does during those parties is not police business."

"That's not entirely true," Daniel said. "We've identified several of the young ladies who attended those parties as paid escorts But we aren't from Vice. We're homicide detectives, and we're here because your club has come up in a homicide investigation. We'd like your help."

"How?" Edna asked.

Daniel took a folder out of his briefcase. He'd put together a six-pack of photographs of middle-aged men and handed the pictures to her, one by one.

"Please look carefully and see if you can identify any of these gentlemen as habitués of your club," Brenda said.

Edna took the photos. "Even if we recognize someone, it won't help you," she said. "We don't know anyone's real name. Everyone uses a fake name here."

She looked at the photos carefully, one at a time, and handed them to her husband.

"Anyone look familiar?" Brenda asked.

Edna nodded. "This is Ted," she said, handing over the photo of Edwin Larramore. "And this is John." She placed the picture of George Taylor on the table.

"Anyone else?" Daniel asked.

Both of them shook their heads. Daniel had included a photo of Oliver Wilson as well.

"Tell us how the club works," Brenda said. "How do people find out about you and join?"

"It's a private club," Nate said. "In order to join, you have to be vouched for by another member. Members pay a fee and are guaranteed to be able to use the club at least twice a month. We only have six couples at a time, so we have to limit the membership."

"Why only six?" Brenda asked.

"Our house only has four bedrooms," Edna said. "Members call and reserve the nights they want. We have parties twice a week, on Wednesday and Saturday. We provide refreshments, free of charge, and clean sheets and towels. Everyone is required to leave by 3:00 a.m."

"I see," Daniel said. "And how do the parties work? What do couples expect to get here?"

"Sex, Detective," Edna said. "Some of our clients like to switch partners. Others like threesomes or foursomes, or get turned on by watching others screw. There's something for everyone."

"Do you have any rules?" Brenda asked.

Edna nodded. "Our members promise complete discretion. If they recognize someone, they're supposed to keep it to themselves. Some of our clients come with their spouses or significant others, but many are married and indulging in a little something extra on the side. We also don't allow any rough stuff. We can't afford to have a client get hurt here. If any member steps out of line, they're expelled."

"Tell us about Ted," Daniel asked. "How long has he been a member?"

Edna pursed her lips and considered the question. "I think he's been coming for about two years. He usually brings a much younger partner. At the beginning, there was lots of variation, but for the past six months, he's been bringing Alice. She's very popular. Gorgeous girl."

"Ever had any complaints or problems about Ted?" Brenda asked.

Nate shook his head. "Perfect gentleman."

"Who referred him?" Daniel asked.

"I don't remember. I think it was one of our female members. We don't keep track of referrals."

"What about John? How long has he been coming?" Daniel asked.

"John's new. I think he's only been here twice. Nancy, his partner, is a member." Edna said.

"Would you be able to tell me if Ted and John were ever at the same party?" Daniel asked.

"That we can do. We keep our reservations on the computer." Nate walked over to a terminal in the corner of the dining room and booted it up. "Here you go. I only see one overlap. It was John's first visit in October."

Daniel walked over and peered at the date. It was a week before the murder. "Can you print that out for me?"

Nate complied. "Can you tell us why you're asking all these questions? If one of these guys is a suspect in a murder case, we don't want him here."

"I'm sorry," Daniel said. "I really can't discuss an ongoing investigation. But you might want to avoid making reservations for either of them, for the time being. You've been very helpful. Thank you."

"Does that mean we won't have any trouble with the Vice division?" Nate asked.

"As I said, we aren't from Vice and there's no reason I can think of, at the moment, to mention your club to them," Daniel said.

Daniel and Brenda left the house and walked across the street to Daniel's car.

"How in the world did you get Vice to check on those women so fast?" Brenda asked. "You must have a friend there who owes you big time."

"I didn't," Daniel said. "Tomorrow morning, I'll have Izzy do background checks on all the car owners and Photoshop the pictures we took. We'll send the ones of the women to Vice and see if they identify any call girls. I didn't want to wait until I had that information to interview the Fitches."

"Daniel Ross, remind me never to play poker with you," Brenda said.

On Monday morning, Daniel updated Izzy on their weekend and downloaded the photos from his camera to Izzy's computer.

"See if you can improve these enough to send the shots of the women to Vice for an ID," Daniel said. "I'd especially like to know the identity of the young woman who came with George Taylor, and check on the owners of the cars we identified. Maybe someone has a connection to Larramore that we don't know about."

Izzy nodded. "I do have one more interesting piece of data for you. You asked me to see if anyone has a UC San

Diego connection. George Taylor got his PhD there in the seventies."

"At the same time that the diarsine paper was written?" Daniel asked.

"Looks like it," Izzy said. "On the other hand, it's a big university. There's no reason to think that Taylor had any connection with J.C. Neuman."

"Maybe not," Daniel said, "but it won't hurt to ask."

Daniel stood in front of the directory for the Physics building and made a note of the location of George Taylor's office.

"I wonder if we'll get another update on the search for the perfect Earth-like planet," Brenda said.

"I don't think so," Daniel said. "George Taylor is an elementary particle physicist."

"Think he's in?"

"I would think so. It's 10:00 a.m."

They took the elevator to the top floor and found a corner office labeled *Physics and Astronomy*. Opening the door led them into a front office with an attractive reception-ist, who was on the phone. She signaled them to wait while she completed her call.

"Can I help you?" she asked.

"I'm Detective Ross of the LAPD. I'm here to see Dr. Taylor."

"Do you have an appointment?"

"No," Daniel said. "But, I'm sure he'll see us. Would you mind notifying him that we're here?"

Just as the receptionist turned on her intercom, Taylor opened his office door and saw them.

"Detectives. This is unexpected. What can I do for you? Have you discovered anything new?" he asked.

Daniel nodded. "We have. We need a few minutes of your time."

Taylor motioned them to follow him into the inner sanctum. His office was at least twice the size of Oliver Wilson's. Two walls with large windows provided a view of the campus. The other two walls were lined with floor-to-ceiling bookcases, loaded with physics books and journals. Daniel imagined that the journals were rapidly becoming obsolete with everything now available online. Taylor had a large, L-shaped desk, a comfortable leather desk chair, a small seating area (consisting of a loveseat and two chairs on a worn oriental rug), and a conference table with seating for six. It was the office of a man who had been there for a long time and liked his comforts.

Taylor deposited himself at the head of the table and Daniel and Brenda seated themselves on either side.

"Dr. Taylor," Daniel began. "You know that we've been investigating the homicide of Dr. Larramore. We've recently learned that he was a regular participant in parties at a swinger's club. You were identified, attending that same club on Saturday night. You were also there a week before Dr. Larramore's death. In fact, you were both at the same party."

Taylor's jaw dropped. "That is absurd. I'd never go to a place like that. Whoever supposedly identified me must have been mistaken."

Brenda, who was taking notes, let out a sigh. "Dr. Taylor, we identified you. We saw you enter the club and we ran the plates on your car. We have your photo. There is no point in denying it. You may as well cooperate with us and answer our questions. Unless you'd prefer to do this down at the station?"

"I would prefer not to do it at all," Taylor said, beginning to stand.

"I'm afraid that isn't an option, sir," Daniel said. "We aren't accusing you of anything. We're just collecting information about Edwin Larramore. If the information turns out not to be relevant to the murder investigation, it need go no further."

Taylor's lips tightened, but he sat down. "What do you want to know?"

"When was the first time you went to the club?" Brenda asked.

"It was in October. I've only been there twice."

"Were you aware that Edwin Larramore was a member?" Daniel asked.

"Of course not," Taylor said. "If I'd known, I'd never have gone. It's not the kind of place where you want to run into acquaintances."

"Did you run into Larramore on that first visit?" Daniel asked.

"Yes, we saw one another."

"Did you have a conversation?" Brenda asked.

"No, we ignored one another. Those are the rules of the club. No one uses their own name, and if you see someone you know, you keep your mouth shut."

"Were you concerned that Larramore wouldn't keep his mouth shut?" Daniel asked.

Taylor shook his head. "Both of us were married. Both of us were there with younger women who weren't our wives. It was a draw. Neither of us could risk saying anything and neither of us could afford a scandal."

"Did you recognize his partner?" Brenda asked.

"The guests had traded partners by the time I'd gotten

there. I didn't know which woman he'd brought and I wasn't paying attention."

"Did either of you say anything to one another afterwards, when you saw each another at work?" Daniel asked.

Taylor shook his head.

"Were you surprised to see him there?" Daniel asked.

"Not really. Edwin had a reputation for screwing around. There were suggestions that he preyed on students, but in the absence of any sexual harassment complaints, I had no grounds to investigate. His being at the club wasn't inconsistent with what I already knew about him."

"Why did you go back to the club, Dr. Taylor," Brenda asked. "Didn't it make you nervous that you had been seen?"

"I wasn't going to go back, but the young lady I was with is a member and really likes it. After Edwin died, I decided I was safe enough. I guess I miscalculated. Are you planning to tell my wife?"

"Why would we do that?" Daniel said. "We're just trying to learn all we can about Edwin Larramore."

"Just one more question, sir," Brenda said. "We understand that you received your PhD at UC San Diego. While you were there, did you come across a chemistry graduate student named Jaycee Neuman?"

Taylor pursed his lips and shook his head. "I don't think so. There wasn't much contact between Physics and Chemistry. We were in different buildings."

"She wasn't someone you dated or knew socially?" Daniel asked.

"The only woman I dated, when I was a graduate student, was my wife Barbara. She was an undergraduate at the time."

"I see. Thanks for your time sir." Daniel said.

Daniel and Brenda entered the outer office. The receptionist was back on the phone. There was something vaguely familiar about her. Daniel took out his phone, pretended to check his messages, and when she looked away, he took a quick photo.

Brenda gave him a quizzical look as they left.

"She looks familiar. When I get back to the office, I want to compare this photo with the shot of Taylor's girlfriend at the club."

Brenda nodded. "Taylor's looking like a good suspect. I'll bet he had a passkey to all the offices, and he certainly has a motive."

"If we can only establish a link to J.C. Neuman, maybe we finally have a suspect with access to the poison," Daniel said.

Hannah would be so pleased that he was turning his investigation in a direction other than Carolyn.

CHAPTER THIRTY-FIVE

I T SEEMED IMPOSSIBLE THAT FOUR WEEKS HAD PASSED since Carolyn Larramore's last official obstetrical exam, but here she was on my schedule for a twenty-eight-week evaluation and ultrasound.

She turned and faced me as I entered the ultrasound room. Her face looked pale and drawn, although she had made an effort to smear some pink lipstick on her mouth. I glanced at her chart. Her blood pressure was 130/90, higher than I liked to see it, and she'd only gained a pound in the past month.

"How are you doing?" I asked.

"Not so great," she replied. "I wanted to talk to you for a few minutes before the ultrasound. My mother's in the waiting room and would like to see the scan. There are a few things she doesn't know about that I'd like to discuss."

"Of course," I said.

"I took your advice."

"What advice was that?" I asked.

"You told me I could obtain Edwin's medical records as the executor of his estate, so I did. It turns out that he'd had a vasectomy before we were married. He knew I was interested in children and he never told me. There's obviously no possibility that my baby was his."

"I'm so sorry," I said. "That must feel like such a betrayal. Have you decided if you're going to tell the man who did father your child?"

"Unfortunately, that choice was taken away from me by the police. They somehow figured out that Oliver was my lover and confronted him. They also told him he was likely responsible for my pregnancy. He was pretty shocked."

"Have the two of you spoken?"

"Oh, yes," Carolyn said. "He came to my office and was the perfect lover. He told me he wanted to be there for me when the baby was born and he offered to extend his stay at the Institute. He also asked me to go back to Australia with him afterwards, so we could try to be a family."

"That's a lot to deal with, all at once," I said. "Are you going to take him up on it?"

"Not without a very good Australian job offer," Carolyn said. "I've already done my time as a powerful man's appendage. I'm not interested in doing that again, with Oliver or anyone else. I told him we should see how we feel about one another over the next few months, until the baby is born, and then we'll revisit the conversation."

"Is there any possibility of a good Australian job offer?" I asked.

"Oliver offered to put me in contact with the chair of the Chemistry department at his campus. I may take him up on it, but not if it means another dead-end, non-tenure track, academic job on another continent. I'm going to start job hunting on my own, as soon as I can generate a little emotional energy. Anyway, I wanted to tell you all of this.

But I haven't told my mother anything yet, so I'd appreciate your discretion."

"Of course." Great, I thought, another secret to juggle. "Shall I ask my nurse to have Jackie come in?"

Carolyn nodded. While we were waiting for Jackie, I took Carolyn's blood pressure again, hoping that it had gone down. It hadn't.

Jackie entered the exam room, all smiles. She hugged Carolyn and thanked me for allowing her to watch. I asked Carolyn to lie down, covered her abdomen with ultrasound gel, and measured her uterus.

"Can you tell the sex?" Jackie asked.

"Yes, of course, but Carolyn wanted it to be a surprise, so we haven't looked. Have you changed your mind?" I asked.

Carolyn shook her head. "Sorry, Mom. You get to find out when your grandchild is born and not a day sooner."

I measured the head diameters, the abdominal circumference and the femur length. Then, I calculated the fetal weight and measured the amount of amniotic fluid. I was not pleased. We had a problem.

"Carolyn, we need to talk," I said. "The baby is very small for 28 weeks. It's in the 10th percentile. You've only gained a pound this month, and the amount of amniotic fluid is lower than I would like. We call this IUGR. It stands for intrauterine growth retardation. Hypertension can cause it, among other things."

"What do we do about it? Do I need to eat more?" she said.

"Yes, you do need to pay attention to your nutrition, and we need to do everything possible to eliminate stress in your life. You may be developing pregnancy-induced hypertension. You're borderline right now. I want to put you on modified bed rest. That means you can get up for meals and to go to the bathroom, but otherwise I want you resting and relaxing. Read a good novel. Watch TV. Put work on hold for awhile."

"Is the baby in danger?" Carolyn asked.

"Not right now," I said. "But we need to watch you carefully. I want you to get a blood pressure cuff at the pharmacy and take your pressure daily. I need to know if it gets above 140/100. I'll be following you with regular exams and scans. We'll keep measuring the baby's size and the amount of fluid. I'll also be looking at the fetal heart rate tracing. If any of those parameters tells me the baby is safer outside than inside, we may choose to deliver you early. But, hopefully, nowhere near this early."

"I'll do whatever it takes," Carolyn said. "The baby is obviously my first priority."

"You can stay at my house," Jackie said. "I have a comfortable guest room and I'll be there to make you breakfast and dinner every day."

"Mom, it's okay. I can manage at home."

"Actually," I said, "it would be a good idea for you not to be alone. You're more likely to observe bed rest if someone is there to do things for you. Why not try it for awhile?"

I wouldn't normally insert myself into a mother-daughter conversation of this sort. I know I wouldn't have opted to stay at my mother's house under similar circumstances. But I also knew Carolyn would cheat if left to her own devices. Bed rest is harder than it sounds.

"Okay, I know when I'm outnumbered," Carolyn said. "Let's stop at my house and pack some things. When do you want to see me again, Dr. Kline?"

"Every two weeks," I said. "Unless your blood pressure goes up before that. Remember, try to avoid anything stressful."

"Easy for you to say," she said. "Tell it to the damn police."

The damn police got home about half-an-hour after I did. I was in the den, with Zoe on my lap. She was reading me an episode of her favorite series, *The Berenstain Bears*. Her reading was becoming increasingly fluent and I was quite proud of her. When she got a little older, I would give her unlimited purchase privileges for books. In my family, everyone reads. I liked historical novels, science fiction and fantasy. Daniel, not surprisingly, was a mystery fan.

"How are my favorite girls?" Daniel said, depositing kisses on both our foreheads.

I looked up and gave him an air kiss. Zoe invited him to sit down and listen to the next chapter.

"I'm just going to wash up and get a cold drink," he said. "And then I'll join you. What's for dinner?"

"Homemade pea soup and Cobb salad," I said. "When you come back down, I'll get dinner together."

Thank God, for Emilia. Getting dinner together meant taking the salad out of the refrigerator and warming up the pot of soup. She'd even set the table for us. Hiring her when Zoe was born had been the smartest thing I'd ever done.

Daniel and Zoe finished off the chapter, we had dinner, and Zoe headed off to her room to do the rest of her homework.

Daniel starting rinsing the dishes and putting them in the dishwasher.

"How was your day?" I asked. "Did you find out anything substantial at the club?"

"Maybe," Daniel said. "We've had a new twist in the

case, thanks to our stakeout, and a new suspect. He's got motive and opportunity, and a possible, although remote, connection to the poison. We'll be following it up."

"Does that mean Carolyn Larramore is off the hook?" I asked.

"No, Hannah. It doesn't," Daniel said.

"Look, Daniel," I said. "Today, I put Carolyn on bed rest for a pregnancy complication I can't discuss with you. The last thing she needs right now, medically, is stress. Can't you just lay off her?"

Daniel turned away from the sink and looked at me. "You know better than that. I don't tell you how to do your job and you can't tell me how to do mine."

"And I respect that. But in this situation, I have to say something. I'm responsible for two patients here, Carolyn and her baby. And the baby has nothing to do with your case."

"And I'm trying to solve a premeditated murder. When a husband is killed, the wife is high on the suspect list. And I don't have enough evidence yet to convince me that she wasn't responsible."

"Fine," I said, slamming the refrigerator door on the leftovers. "If you guys continue to harass her, and she winds up with a preterm delivery and a kid in the NICU, it'll be on your head."

I stormed out of the kitchen. Men were so unreasonable.

Daniel sighed, put some detergent in the dishwasher, and started the cycle. No point in following Hannah out of the room. She'd calm down eventually and see that he was right. Or maybe she wouldn't. He had to admit, the last time she insisted that his top murder suspect hadn't done it, she'd been right. She was an accurate judge of character. Perhaps it was that kind of intuition that made her such a good doctor.

He opened the freezer door and took out some chocolate chip ice cream. Grabbing a spoon, he started eating it out of the container, as he contemplated his next moves. He needed to identify the woman who'd gone to the club with George Taylor and see if Taylor had been telling the truth about his interaction with Larramore. They should also interview Barbara, George's wife. Any connection with Jaycee Neuman was probably a long shot, but it wouldn't hurt to check. In the meantime, he could put Carolyn on hold. Getting a search warrant for her laboratory would no doubt increase Carolyn's stress and aggravate Hannah. And that would increase his stress.

I went upstairs to Zoe's room and reviewed her math homework. Being in her presence always calmed me down and cheered me up. She put on her pajamas, insisted on reading me another *Berenstain Bears* book, and kissed me goodnight. Our night-time ritual of snuggling and reading was my favorite. I hoped she'd grow up to be as voracious a reader as I was. I tucked her in, turned out the light, and retreated to the master bedroom.

I could hear the television in the den, which meant that Daniel wasn't coming up any time soon. I booted up my laptop and thought about what I knew. The key to this whole case was the chemical, and Daniel had only one link to it, the authors of a paper written in the 1970's. He'd already interviewed a ninety-year-old retired professor, who clearly wasn't a suspect, but he'd been unable to locate the graduate student who was the real expert.

J.C. Neuman's first name couldn't be Jaycee. That had to be a nickname. I contemplated that for awhile. If J.C. was a graduate student in the 1970's, then she was probably born in the 1950's. I searched for the most popular girl's names for that decade. The C could be a middle name, or a maiden name.

There were a dozen names beginning with J in the top 200, several of which were just variations on the same name. I focused on the ones that began with JA. There was Janice, Jane, and Jacqueline.

I knew if J.C. had done any more academic research, those papers would have been published under her last name and initials. But Daniel had already told me that there were no more research publications. Perhaps she'd gotten married and changed her name, or perhaps Neuman was a married name and she'd gotten divorced.

I decided on a three-pronged attack. Marriage and divorce were public documents and accessible online. I could search under all those name variations. I wondered if Facebook would be helpful. Unfortunately, I wasn't on Facebook. Social media seemed to be a full-time job. But my nurse was a Facebook enthusiast. I'd get her to log in, so I could go sleuthing in the morning. I could get to the office early and continue my search during my lunch break.

I suddenly realized that I could no longer hear the television, which meant that Daniel was on his way up. I quickly shut down the laptop. There was no need for him to know that I was snooping into his case, unless I came up with something useful.

As Daniel entered the room, Hannah looked up from her laptop. She wasn't smiling, but she wasn't glaring at him either. They'd never had an argument before, and Daniel wasn't quite sure of how to proceed.

"I guess I overreacted," he said. "We're both just trying to do our jobs, and they don't usually come into conflict. Sorry."

"Your job is endangering my patient," Hannah said. "I'm worried about Carolyn's baby. If the situation wasn't serious, I wouldn't have brought it up."

Daniel nodded. "I know. I can't ignore information that leads to Carolyn, but right now, I've got some other possibilities to investigate. How about I give you a head's up if I have to refocus on her? At least that way you'll be prepared obstetrically."

"If that's the best you can do," Hannah said. "I'm used to us functioning as a team, not at cross purposes. It's frustrating."

"I know it is," he said. "Why don't we get some sleep? Maybe it will feel better in the morning."

CHAPTER THIRTY-SIX

DANIEL WAS WAITING FOR IZZY TO FINISH COLLECTING all the data from the swingers club stakeout before proceeding. Vice had taken awhile to identify the women.

"Okay," Izzy said, looking up from his computer. "We've got four guys identified. One you know about. None of the other three have any obvious connection to Larramore. We've got a restaurant owner from Ventura, an accountant from Costa Mesa, and the last one's a BMW dealer in Calabasas. Two of the three were with professional escorts, identified by Vice."

"What about the girl with Taylor?" Daniel asked.

"Taylor's partner is a girl named Michelle Benton. The photo you took outside the club is a good match for the one of Taylor's receptionist. Reckless of him to fool around with an employee, but he probably wasn't thinking with anything above his neck. The girl has no prior record. She's a recent junior college graduate. I hope that helps." Izzy grinned.

Daniel thought he had the whitest, straightest teeth he'd ever seen. Perhaps it was the contrast with his black skin.

"I could never solve anything without you," Daniel said.

Daniel sat at his desk, trying to decide how best to approach Taylor's receptionist. He definitely didn't want to go to the office, and he didn't want to warn her by calling first. It was never a good idea to allow a witness time to think over what they were going to tell you.

"Why don't we head over to the Institute just before lunch and hope she leaves the building?" he finally said to Brenda.

"Sounds good," she said. "I can watch the back exit and you can keep tabs on the front door."

At exactly ten minutes past noon, Michelle Benton left the Physics building. She was wearing a long, fuzzy gray sweater and black slacks and carrying a large red purse. Her long dark hair, pulled back into a ponytail, swung as she walked. She was humming to herself as she found an empty bench, under a tree, in one of the campus gardens. She took out a sandwich from her purse, as well as a paperback book, and settled down with her lunch.

Daniel and Brenda strolled over.

"Miss Benton?" Brenda asked.

Michelle looked up.

"May we have a word?"

"You're the two detectives who were in the office, talking to Dr. Taylor," she said.

"That's right. Can we sit down?" Daniel asked.

Michelle moved over to the end of the bench, leaving them room to sit without flanking her.

"What do you want?" she asked.

"We just have a few questions for you," Daniel said. "We know you accompanied your boss, last Saturday night, to a private swingers club in Van Nuys. We know you were also there with him in October. We're interested in what you can tell us about that first visit."

"Why are you interested in George's sex life? Did he tell you that he went with me to the club?" she asked.

"He did not. He politely referred to you as a young lady," Daniel said. "But we have photographs of the two of you entering the club. Tell us how long you've worked for Dr. Taylor."

"About two years," Michelle said.

"And how long have you been having an affair with him?" Brenda asked.

"I'm not sure I'd dignify our relationship by calling it an affair. George is a sweet man who craves a little adventure to brighten up an otherwise conventional life. I provide it, but it's not some great love. He's hardly my only sexual partner," she said.

"Did you introduce him to the club? Are you a member?" Daniel asked.

"I did. And yes, I've belonged for about a year. It's an interesting change of pace," she said.

"Tell us about the first time you took Dr. Taylor there. Did he meet anyone he recognized?"

Her eyebrows tightened in thought. Finally, she nodded. "I think so. When we first entered the living room, there were several other couples there. George tensed up. I thought, at the time, it was just because he was new, and perhaps a little uncomfortable."

"Did something happen later to make you think there was more to it?" Daniel asked.

"Yes. We socialized for a few minutes, and then paired

up with another couple for a foursome. When we were done, the other couple left the room, and George said he needed to go the bathroom, which was down the hall. I was still getting dressed. After a few moments, I heard his voice and that of another man. I couldn't make out what they were saying but the tone was angry. The conversation was short, and George came back, looking upset."

"Did you see the other man?" Brenda asked.

Michelle shook her head. "I asked George what was wrong, but he avoided my question. We didn't see anyone when we left."

"When was the next time you went to the club with him?" Brenda asked.

"Not until last Saturday. I was there a few times with other partners, but George seemed reluctant, and I didn't pressure him. The foursome seemed to really turn him on, so I assumed it had something to do with the man he'd been talking to. Last week, he asked me if we could go again. Is George in trouble because of the club?"

"No, not at all," Daniel reassured her. "You've been helpful. Thank you."

"Periodically," said Brenda, as they strolled across campus, "listening to those twenty-somethings talk about their sex lives astonishes me. It's not that I'm a prude or anything, but there's something about having random sex with people whose names you don't even know that bothers me."

Daniel laughed. "We're just two old relics," he said, "trapped in a Puritan culture."

"Maybe I grew up reading too many romance novels," Brenda said. "Who would have predicted hook-up apps on your cell phone? People don't even have foreplay nowadays, they just text."

Brenda waited for Daniel to open his car door. "What did you think of Michelle?"

"I think she was telling us all she knew. Obviously, George lied when he said that he and Larramore had no interaction with one another. He's looking better and better as a suspect."

"So, shall we drop in on Barbara Taylor and see what she has to say?" Brenda asked.

"First, we need lunch," Daniel said. "Watching Michelle finish off that sandwich made me hungry."

After a meatball sandwich for Daniel and a Caesar salad for Brenda, the two of them drove to the Taylor home. Daniel rang the doorbell, which was answered promptly by Barbara Taylor.

He thought she looked like the prototype of an older faculty wife. There was no makeup on her plump, pleasant face and her gray hair was styled in a practical short cut. She wore a light blue cashmere twin set and gray slacks. A pair of reading glasses on a gold ribbon hung around her neck. She had cautiously left the chain on her door.

"Yes?" she asked, in a tone of voice reserved for visits from Jehovah's Witnesses.

Daniel showed her his badge. "Mrs. Taylor. I'm Daniel Ross, the lead detective in the Edwin Larramore case. This is my partner, Brenda Jordan. Might we have a word for a few minutes?"

Barbara took Daniel's ID from his hand and examined it with care. This was one cautious woman. Finally, she nodded, removed the chain and invited them into her living room.

The house was an old English Revival with diamond-paned leaded windows, dark wood floors, and a tall, elaborately carved fireplace. A sofa and two arm chairs, upholstered in cheerful floral fabric, faced the fire. Daniel was paying more attention to houses these days, ever since Hannah had given him a brief architectural education.

"Are you sure you don't want to talk to my husband?" she asked.

"We have spoken to him. He was very helpful. We're hoping you might have something to add," Daniel said.

Barbara sat down on what was clearly her favorite armchair. There was an open book and a cup of tea on the side table. She nodded toward the sofa.

"Can I get either of you something to drink?" she asked.

"That's kind of you, but we just had lunch," Brenda said. "We won't keep you long."

"Mrs. Taylor, we understand that you did your undergraduate degree at UC San Diego," Daniel said.

Barbara nodded.

"While you were there, did you, by any chance, come across a student named Jaycee Neuman?" he asked.

Her forehead furrowed in thought and she didn't respond for awhile. "There's something familiar about the name, Detective. Let me see if she was in my undergraduate class."

Barbara got up and went to a large bookcase, which covered one whole wall of the living room. She scanned it rapidly, and retrieved a leather-covered volume from one of the lower shelves. Sitting down, she flipped through it.

"I see a Newberg, and a Newton, but no Neuman in my yearbook," she said.

"She wouldn't have been in your class," Brenda said. "She was a graduate student in chemistry at about the same time you were there."

Sudden light dawned in Barbara's eyes. "Now, I remember why that name is so familiar," she said. "Jaycee was my Freshman Chemistry T.A."

"T.A.?" Brenda asked.

"Teaching assistant. The lecture classes in freshman science are huge, so they break them up into smaller units, each taught by a graduate student, so that you can go over the homework assignments and ask questions. I particularly remember Jaycee because she was the only female T.A."

"What was she like?" Daniel asked.

"Very smart. Very tough. She had to be, to hold her own with some of the wiseass guys in our section," Barbara said.

"Were you friends?" Brenda asked.

"Hardly. I was a freshman and she was a graduate student. I wasn't a Chemistry major. I only took Freshman Chemistry to satisfy my science requirement. We had nothing in common. Besides, I was spending all my free time with George."

"Do you remember what she looked like?" Daniel asked.

Barbara thought for awhile, leaning back and closing her eyes. "It's hard to remember. It was so long ago, I can't image her face at all. She was slim and pretty, with long, light brown hair. The thing I remember most about her was that she was wearing a huge diamond engagement ring, and a wedding band that was almost as glitzy. I was paying attention to engagement rings in those days, and I thought she must have married a very rich guy."

Brenda laughed.

"May I ask why you're interested in Jaycee Neuman?"

Barbara said. "I don't see how she could possibly be involved in your case."

"We're trying to trace her because we think she has some pertinent scientific information, and we haven't been able to find her so far. We're talking to everyone who went to UC San Diego, who might have known her. Would you have any idea of where she went when she graduated?" Daniel asked.

Barbara shook her head. "Sorry, I never saw her again after the class was over."

Daniel stood up and held out his hand. "Thank you for taking the time, Mrs. Taylor. We appreciate it."

"Well, we've learned one useful thing," Brenda said. "Jaycee was married."

"Actually, I knew that," Daniel said. "Professor McKenzie mentioned that she and her husband moved to the East Coast."

"I have a feeling she's the key to this case. We've got to find her. If she was married, and Neuman was her married name, maybe she got divorced and all the hunting we've been doing has been under the wrong name."

"I'll bet you're right," Daniel said. "Let's ask Izzy to start checking divorce records from the 1970's and 1980's. Maybe we can figure out what name she's using now."

CHAPTER THIRTY-SEVEN

I WAS SITTING AT MY DESK, JUGGLING A LUNCH OF blueberry yogurt with a national computer database of divorce decrees. It was really remarkable what one could find online. Everything seemed to be in the public domain.

I'd spent a fruitless hour, early this morning, on Facebook, thanks to my nurse, who was a social media maven. I had no idea how she found the time. We looked up Jaycee Neuman, and all the Neumans that we could find with the first names on my list. There was a Jaycee Newman, and quite a few women whose first names were popular in the fifties. We scanned their photos, looking for women of the appropriate age who might be the elusive J.C. Fortunately, my mother's generation wasn't all that common on Facebook, so I was only left with a handful of possibilities. Unfortunately, I wasn't able to access many of their pages for more information. Apparently, older Facebook users were more concerned about privacy than Generation X, so unless I was a "friend," I couldn't go any further. I printed a list of the possibilities, thinking I could check them out on alternate databases.

Public records were more forthcoming. After searching "divorce decrees United States," I found several free databases that not only supplied divorce information, but would give you birth and death certificates, marriage licenses, felony convictions and sexual predator information. I applied the same strategy to the divorce decrees. There was no Jaycee, but I got a number of female Neumans who had been divorced all over the country. I printed the list and proceeded to look up the actual documents. The decree supplied the maiden name, which I could then, in a separate window, crosscheck with the birth certificate, to see if the woman was the right age. This was a tedious process until I got to page two.

A Jacqueline Neuman had divorced her husband, Robert Neuman, in New York, in 1984. Mrs. Neuman's maiden name was Cantor. I checked the birth certificate, and the age was right for Jackie. I looked for a birth certificate under Carolyn Neuman, and the data matched.

Could it be that simple? Just to triple check, I looked up Edwin Larramore's marriage certificate and found that he had married Carolyn Neuman seven years ago. I finished my yogurt.

I didn't believe in coincidence. The key question was, if Jackie Cantor, our realtor, was J.C., and had the nickel diarsine, had she used it herself to murder her abusive son-in-law? Or had Carolyn obtained it from her without her knowledge? Or had the two of them planned the murder together?

The second most important question was, should I pass this information on to Daniel?

I knew what he would do. He'd get a search warrant for Jackie's home and office, and for Carolyn's laboratory, and bring both of them in for questioning. I couldn't think of anything that would create more stress on the baby.

I knew I had to tell him eventually, but before I did, I had to be absolutely certain that Jackie and J.C. were the same person. I was pretty sure I could find a way to search the Cantor household without causing any undue alarms.

CHAPTER THIRTY-EIGHT

"ANY LUCK?" DANIEL ASKED IZZY.

"I'm working on it. I've found about a dozen women whose first name begins with J and whose middle or maiden name begins with C. I'll weed it down to those in the appropriate age range, and do a background check on the ones who are left. Maybe we'll luck out," Izzy said.

"How long do you think it'll take?" Daniel asked. He was feeling antsy and wanted answers yesterday.

"It will take as long as it takes. I'll call you when I'm done. In the meantime, go away and detect something. I hate it when you guys hang over my shoulder."

"Sorry," Daniel said.

Maybe he and Brenda should go confront George Taylor again. Clearly, he'd lied to them, but without any proof as to how he could have obtained the poison, they wouldn't really get anywhere. And if they pushed him too hard, too soon, he'd lawyer up. Hannah's job was so much easier. She always pulled off a happy ending.

—————————

CHAPTER THIRTY-NINE

M Y OPPORTUNITY TO VISIT JACKIE'S HOUSE CAME THE next day, with a call from Carolyn.

"Dr. Kline, you told me to call if my blood pressure went up. It's 150/100. I've checked it three times this morning."

"Any headaches or nausea?" I asked.

"No, just high blood pressure," she said. "Would you like me to come in?"

"How far from my office is your mother's house?" I asked.

"She's in Bel Air. I can be there in twenty minutes, or half an hour, depending on the traffic on Sunset," she said.

"I have a better idea," I said. "Bel Air is on my way home. Why don't I stop by with my portable ultrasound later this afternoon? My last two patients just rescheduled, so I can be there by about 3:30. You don't need the stress of driving in traffic. Is that okay?"

"That would be great," she said. She gave me her mother's address and signed off.

I finished at the office shortly before 3:00 p.m., and packed a bag with everything I would need to examine

Carolyn at home. I told my receptionist to text me in exactly forty-five minutes with an office update, and headed for Bel Air.

Jackie lived in the slightly less costly region of Bel Air, on a small street just off Roscomare Road. The house was one-story and contemporary, with a charming garden at the front, shaded by large maple trees.

I rang the bell.

Carolyn came to the door, wearing a peach silk dressing gown, belted beneath her breasts and emphasizing her abdomen. She smiled a greeting and told me to follow her to her room.

We walked through an airy, bright living room, furnished with contemporary sofas mixed with antique tables and accessories. The accessories looked genuine and expensive to my, admittedly untutored, eye.

The guest room featured a sophisticated floral wallpaper with a matching duvet and two comfortable chairs. The large side table was loaded with books, a water pitcher and glass, a blood pressure cuff, and a cell phone.

Carolyn fluffed her pillows, removed her robe, and got back into bed.

"Lovely room," I commented. "Your mother has excellent taste."

"She does," Carolyn said. "This was my room when I lived here. I've always liked it."

I took my blood pressure cuff out from my bag and rechecked her pressure. I was hoping she'd made a mistake, but she hadn't. I was not happy. Just then, right on schedule, my cell phone chirped, letting me know there was a text. I took it out and checked it.

"Carolyn, my office needs me to call them urgently. The

cell reception here isn't great. Do you, by any chance, have a landline I could borrow?"

"Sure," she said. "My mother's study has one. It's just across the hall."

This was just what I was hoping for.

I returned to my medical bag and took out a sterile urine cup. "While I'm on the phone, do you think you could get a urine sample for me? It doesn't have to be much. I just want to test it for protein."

Carolyn got obediently out of bed, took the cup and headed to her bathroom.

I exited her bedroom, closed the door, and found Jackie's study. I put on a pair of latex gloves, which I'd stashed in my pocket, and closed the study door behind me. If Daniel searched this place, I didn't want my fingerprints anywhere they weren't supposed to be.

∼

Jackie's study was furnished in Early American reproduction furniture. There was a graceful, mahogany desk and bookcase, and a comfortable wing chair with an ottoman. One whole wall was devoted to photographs and laminated degrees. I checked that out first. Her real estate license was at eye level, along with several mother-daughter pictures, and photos of Jackie with Los Angeles celebrities. Further down, were her college degrees: her undergraduate degree from UCLA and a PhD in Chemistry from UCSD.

I inwardly groaned. I had really been hoping that I was wrong. The last thing Carolyn needed was the cops breathing down Jackie's neck.

I scanned the bookcase quickly. It had real estate reference books, art books featuring Los Angeles architecture, a bottom shelf with computer software and a black, leather-bound book without a title on the spine. I removed it and looked at the title page. It was Jacqueline Cantor Neuman's PhD thesis on Nickel Diarsine. I flipped through it. There were lots of incomprehensible mathematical equations. Who would have imagined that Jackie could have produced them?

I'd found the key to Daniel's case. Now all I had to do was decide when to tell him. And figure out how just how angry he was going to be for each day I put it off.

I spent a few quick minutes going through Jackie's desk, and the drawers and cabinets in her bathroom, but I didn't find anything that looked like a deadly poison. No point in trying to do the rest of Daniel's job for him. I'd done enough.

I heard the front door slam, and Jackie's voice calling out. I stripped my gloves and opened the bedroom door, just as Carolyn said, "We're in here, Mom."

"You're just in time for the ultrasound," I said, my heart racing at the close call. "Carolyn's blood pressure is a little high, so I stopped over on my way home."

"I didn't know you made house calls," Jackie said.

"Only for special patients."

I took out my urine dipsticks and tested for protein. There was quite a lot, which was another change since I'd tested her in the office, less than a week ago. She was developing pre-eclampsia and doing it quickly.

I unpacked my portable ultrasound and squeezed gel onto Carolyn's belly. The baby was breech, and the amount of amniotic fluid had decreased substantially. I got an estimate of the fetal weight, which continued to be in the 10th percentile. Then, I watched for fetal breathing and movements. Both were there, but not as active as I would like. I was going to have to admit Carolyn to the hospital.

"What's wrong?" Carolyn said. "I can tell by your face that you aren't happy."

"We have several problems, Carolyn, and they add up to the need for delivery. You are rapidly developing severe pre-eclampsia, a combination of high blood pressure and protein in your urine, which won't resolve until the pregnancy is over."

"Is Carolyn in danger?" Jackie asked.

"She could be, if we allow the pre-eclampsia to progress. In its severe form it can produce seizures or liver damage."

"But the baby is only 29 weeks," Carolyn said. "That's so premature."

"It is," I said. "But remember, I told you that if it looked as if the baby would be safer outside than inside, we would have to act. My ultrasound shows a dramatic decrease in the amount of amniotic fluid. That means the blood flow to the placenta has diminished. We need to get the baby out before either of you gets into significant trouble."

"What's your plan?" Jackie asked, moving over to the bed and reaching for Carolyn's hand.

"I'm going to call the hospital and admit her to our Ante-natal Care Unit. We'll put the baby on continuous heart rate monitoring and I'll administer steroids to mature its lungs. We can deliver by Caesarian Section, twenty-four hours after the steroid dose. I'll have our perinatal and neonatal specialists consult as well."

"Do I have to have a C-Section?" Carolyn asked. She was biting her lip and her hands were shaking.

"I'm afraid so. The baby is breech, and even if it weren't, I wouldn't want to subject it to the stress of labor. It'll be painless, and you'll be awake with an epidural, so you can see your baby immediately."

I turned to Jackie. "May I use your landline? I need to call the hospital."

"Of course. There's one in the kitchen. Follow me," she said.

"Mom, while you're there, I could use a cup of herbal tea," Carolyn said.

Jackie leaned down, brushed her daughter's hair from her forehead, and kissed her gently. "Of course, sweetheart, and don't worry. I'll be with you every minute from now until that baby is safely delivered."

Ensconced in Jackie's kitchen, at a small, built-in desk space, I arranged for Carolyn to be admitted, and called in all the appropriate orders. Since I didn't know exactly what time she would receive her steroids, I played it safe and scheduled the C-section for 7:30 a.m., the day after tomorrow. I decided I could wait to talk to Daniel until after the delivery. He might be really angry at me, but I wasn't about to share any information about Carolyn's mom until that baby was out.

CHAPTER FORTY

D ANIEL WAS AT HIS DESK, DOING PAPERWORK FOR A few of his other cases, when Izzy motioned him over.

"I've got a few possibilities," he said. "But only one who currently lives in Los Angeles. And, if I'm not mistaken, she's your victim's mother-in-law."

Brenda looked up from her desk. "No shit," she said.

"Jacqueline Cantor Neuman," Izzy said.

"Well, it's unlikely she synthesized Nickel Diarsine in her real estate office," Brenda said. "So, she must have saved some from her days as a graduate student."

"If she had access, Carolyn certainly would have had access, and possibly her lover, Oliver, as well," Daniel said. "I wonder if this was a joint project, or if only one of them is responsible."

"I'll start working on the warrants," Brenda said. "I assume you'll want to search Jackie's house and Carolyn's lab? Shall we bring them both in for questioning?"

Damn it, Daniel thought. The timing couldn't have been worse. He was going to have to make good on his promise to give Hannah a head's up before he acted. She was going to be livid.

"Let's wait until we have the warrants in hand," Daniel said. "I happen to know that Carolyn Larramore is on bed rest at her mother's house. She's having some complications with her pregnancy. I don't think either of them is likely to leave the country, any time soon."

CHAPTER FORTY-ONE

Aﬀter I arranged hospital admission for Carolyn, and a cot for Jackie, who wanted to spend the night in her daughter's room, I left them gathering together Carolyn's birth bag for the hospital, and Jackie's overnight items, and headed home. Jackie promised she'd get Carolyn to Los Angeles Memorial Hospital within the hour.

I arrived home before Daniel, said goodbye to Emilia, put our chicken dinner in the warming oven, and settled down in the den to watch cartoons with Zoe. Daniel walked in about half-an-hour later. He gave us both hugs, and offered to help me set the table. I could tell from the expression on his face that there was something on his mind.

"I promised you a head's up, if anything involving Carolyn came up in the investigation," he said.

"Has it?" I asked, feeling faintly nauseous.

"Izzy finally tracked down J.C. Neuman. The initials stand for Jacqueline Cantor. She divorced a guy named Robert Neuman in 1984. She's our link to the poison that killed Edwin Larramore."

I decided I'd better confess. "I have something to tell you as well. I just came from making a house call on Carolyn, because her condition is deteriorating. I was answering a text from my office, in Jackie's study, when I noticed her diplomas on the wall. There was a PhD in chemistry from UCSD with the name Jacqueline Cantor Neuman on it."

Daniel's mouth tightened. I could tell he was thinking through what I had just said and he didn't look happy about it.

"Damn it, Hannah. Do you really think I'm so stupid that I can't tell when you're lying to me? I know how smart you are and how your mind works. Do you really expect me to believe that you found that PhD degree accidentally? Look me in the eye and tell me you didn't suspect Jackie ahead of time and go to her house to snoop?" He glared at me.

I sighed. "Guilty as charged. I'm sorry."

"Sorry isn't adequate," he said. "What if I hadn't reached the same conclusion today? When were you planning on telling me? And if you suspected Jackie of murder, did it occur to you, for one minute, that you might not be safe in her house?"

"I was planning to tell you as soon as I delivered Carolyn's baby. She's in the hospital. I just admitted her to the Antenatal Care Unit. She's scheduled for a Caesarian section at 7:30 a.m., the day after tomorrow. Jackie is with her."

Daniel's face flushed, angrier than I had ever seen him before–at least, angrier than he had ever been at me.

"What are you planning to do?"

"I'm going to bring both of them in for questioning. I have search warrants for Jackie's office and home, and Carolyn's lab."

"Daniel, please. You can't bring Carolyn in for questioning, not until after her delivery, when it's medically safe. Jackie is planning to be with her in the operating room during the surgery. Neither of them has any reason to imagine that the police are about to question them again. Can't you just wait until the baby is safely in the NICU? There are three people involved here, and one of them is a fetus."

"We've had this discussion before, Hannah."

"I know. But this investigation has been going on for over two months now. Another few days shouldn't make any difference."

"Whether it makes a difference or not is my decision, not yours. If you can't help me, then you need to stay out of my cases. You do realize, don't you, that this means that one or both of them are guilty? And you're asking me to look the other way, because it's not convenient for the murderer to be brought in right now?"

"It's not like they have tickets to Pantages. Daniel, I'm begging you not to do anything that will put an innocent baby at risk, before delivery."

I still had trouble believing that Carolyn was capable of murder, but you can never know what a person will do when pushed to the limit. If Carolyn was guilty, what would happen to her baby? I didn't want to think about it.

"I can't believe you were going to wait two days to tell me. So, it was okay for me to give you a head's up, as long as you don't have to reciprocate? I trust you, but you don't trust me? Is that how it goes? How would you have liked it, if I had given you a head's up, two days after I brought them in?"

I could feel my face flush. "I'm sorry. Thank you for the

heads up, Daniel. Thank you for trusting me. Can we both just calm down and have dinner?"

"I'm not hungry," he said, storming out of the kitchen and heading upstairs.

CHAPTER FORTY-TWO

Daniel called the station and made arrangements for someone to keep an eye on Jackie's home, and for someone else to tail her if she left the hospital. Then he called Brenda with an update.

"You sound really pissed at Hannah," she said.

"I am. But we're going to have to wait," he said. "Questioning a high-risk pregnant woman in the hospital borders on police brutality."

"What about the searches?" Brenda asked.

"We'll need to wait on those too, until we can question both of them," he said. "I don't want to warn either one, especially Jackie. As soon as that baby is safely in the NICU, we'll bring Jackie in, and I'll pay a hospital visit to Carolyn."

"Okay," Brenda said. "If that's how you want to play it. What about Oliver Wilson? Shouldn't we keep an eye on him as well? If Jackie was the source of the poison, and this murder was a joint project, he could be involved as well."

"Good idea," Daniel said. "I'll set up another tail. What we could use now is a confession."

"Or a bottle of Nickel Diarsine in Jackie's bedroom," Brenda said. "Are you sure you don't want to strike now?"

"Despite what Hannah thinks, I don't want to risk endangering that baby. I think we can be patient for one more day."

CHAPTER FORTY-THREE

I MADE ROUNDS ON CAROLYN, FIRST THING IN THE morning. Her blood pressure was stable at 150/100, the fetal heart rate monitor showed a reassuring strip, and she had received her first dose of steroids at 8:00 PM the previous night.

Daniel had left the house while I was in the shower. He was barely speaking to me. I'd never seen him so angry and I didn't know what to do about it. I also didn't know if he was going to wait for the delivery, or make a move today. The whole situation was making me feel agitated. I'd never seen Daniel lose his temper before, and I was beginning to wonder if I really knew him as well as I thought I did.

I twisted my engagement ring around my finger. Had I made a terrible mistake? Was I so mesmerized by the great sex, and so needy for adult companionship, that I'd committed to marrying the wrong man?

Carolyn was awake and having breakfast when I entered the room. There was no sign of Jackie, but the cot had clearly been slept in.

"How are you this morning," I asked.

Carolyn shrugged. "I feel okay, but I'm scared."

"Scared for the baby?" I asked.

"Part of me is terrified that the baby will die, or have some horrible post birth complication. Another part of me is terrified of being a mother. I feel as if I have no idea what it takes to care for an infant."

I sat down on the edge of her bed. "So far, the baby is looking stable. You should know that the odds of death are very small. We have a fabulous NICU, and they do a great job with premature infants who are over 28 weeks gestation."

"I've been reading stuff on the internet. What if the baby has a brain hemorrhage, or permanent lung disease, or cerebral palsy?" she asked.

"Carolyn, please stop consulting the internet. It will just raise your blood pressure. It's true that any of those complications can happen, but the odds of them happening to your baby are small. I'm arranging for one of the neonatologists to come and answer your questions."

I reached over and squeezed Carolyn's hand.

"The baby will be in the NICU until it is breathing normally, able to feed, and is large enough to go home. That means there will be lots of time for you to learn what to do, under the supervision of the best baby nurses in the hospital. Any woman who can write a PhD thesis can manage to figure out when to change a diaper."

She laughed.

"Speaking of mothering, where's Jackie this morning?" I asked.

"I sent her home to shower, change and have some decent coffee," Carolyn said. "I appreciate her being with me, but I needed a few hours to myself. For one thing, I have to call Oliver."

"Have you told Jackie about him?" I asked.

She shook her head. "You, and of course the police, are the only ones who know. I've decided to put Edwin's name on the birth certificate."

"Can I ask why?" I said.

"I'm a very private person, Dr. Kline, and frankly, I'm scared of the media. Can you just see the headline? WIFE OF MURDERED NOBEL PRIZE WINNER GIVES BIRTH TO LOVER'S CHILD. I'd feel humiliated."

"I understand," I said. "What are you going to say to Oliver?"

"I don't think he'll appreciate a media feeding frenzy either. I'll ask him to come and visit after the baby is born, preferably when Jackie isn't here. If he and I wind up together, we can always arrange for him to adopt our child."

"I see you've thought it all out," I said. "Are you going to want your mother in the operating room with you for the delivery?"

"Absolutely," Carolyn said. "She wouldn't miss it for the world. Jackie's always been a great mom. I only hope I can be as good a parent to my child, as she was to me."

"It sounds as if she's given you a good role model for being a single mother," I said.

"Mom and I have been a team since I was four years old. There's nothing we wouldn't do for one another," Carolyn said.

I wondered if that included collaborating on a murder. I put the thought aside. The murder was Daniel's problem now. I had to let go of it.

"I'll be here first thing tomorrow morning for your delivery," I said.

CHAPTER FORTY-FOUR

S ITTING AND WAITING UNTIL TOMORROW TO BREAK THE Larramore case was driving Daniel crazy. There was nothing he could do, except wait for phone calls from the guys he had tailing Jackie and Oliver.

Brenda brought in chocolate croissants and lattes to distract him. "Maybe you should go to the gym, or practice your shooting. You're practically vibrating in place."

"You're probably right," Daniel said. "Waiting is so much harder than acting."

"Any news?" she asked.

"Jackie left the hospital at 8:00 a.m., and went home. According to the guys watching her house, she's still there. They'll let me know if she leaves."

"And Oliver?"

"In his office."

"Let's go over the plan for tomorrow," Brenda said.

"We wait until the delivery is over and Jackie returns home. We send one team to her office and one to her house. We'll take her in for questioning, as soon as we're done searching. Hopefully, we'll find something useful, or get some information out of her before she calls a lawyer." Daniel said.

"Do you want me to take the lead in bringing Jackie in?" Brenda asked. "Are you still keeping a low profile?"

"After Carolyn delivers, it won't matter if they learn about the connection between me and Hannah. I'm supposed to be running this investigation. I need to be there."

"Okay," Brenda said. "We should get Jackie's fingerprints when we bring her in. We still have one unidentified print on the coffee bag."

Daniel nodded. "Hopefully, Jackie will be exhausted and go home for awhile after the delivery."

"Perhaps," Brenda suggested, "you could ask Hannah to encourage her to do just that."

"I'm leaving Hannah out of it," Daniel said.

By an unspoken, mutual agreement, he and Hannah avoided discussing the murder when he went home that evening. He didn't want anything she told him to wind up compromising his case.

CHAPTER FORTY-FIVE

I WAS HOPING FOR A SOLID NIGHT'S SLEEP BEFORE having to get up at 6:00 a.m. for my 7:30 a.m. surgery. It was not to be. At a little past midnight, my cell phone rang. It was one of the residents.

"Dr. Kline, Mrs. Larramore's fetal monitor strip is starting to show some deep variable decelerations. We scanned her and she has literally no fluid left. Would you like to do the Caesarian now?"

"Absolutely," I said. "Bring her to Labor and Delivery, have an operating room set up, start her on the usual dose of magnesium sulfate so she doesn't have a seizure, and notify the neonatal team. I'll be there in about twenty minutes."

Daniel rolled over. "What's happening?" he asked.

"Baby's in trouble. I'm going in to deliver Carolyn now. I should be home by 4:00 a.m. or so, but if I'm not, could you make sure Zoe gets to school on time? Jan, next door, is driving carpool tomorrow, so you can drop Zoe off at her house if you have to leave early."

"Sure," Daniel said. "Any estimate of when Carolyn will be available for questioning?"

I stripped off my nightgown, put on some underwear and found a pair of scrubs in my dresser drawer. "Carolyn will be in post-op for several hours, until we're certain she's stable. She won't get a room on the OB ward until late morning. I'm planning to put her on IV narcotic medication for pain, for at least twenty-four hours, so you won't be able to talk to her until she's narcotic-free."

Daniel didn't look pleased with my answer, but that was his problem. Mine was getting that baby safely delivered.

I ran a brush through my hair and washed my face with cold water. Then I slipped into my clogs, grabbed my purse, and headed downstairs to my car.

As soon as Daniel heard the front door close, he got on the phone to the guys who were tailing Jackie and gave them an update.

"Let me know as soon as you see her leave the hospital. I'll get the search team together."

He turned off his phone and lay back on his pillows. He hoped he could get some sleep. Tomorrow was going to be a busy day. On the plus side, at least he wasn't the one driving to the hospital and having to operate in the middle of the night.

CHAPTER FORTY-SIX

THE RESIDENTS WERE READY FOR ME WHEN I GOT TO the hospital. Carolyn was prepped and draped, and lying on the operating table, her epidural anesthesia in place. The scrub tech and circulating nurses were in the room, and the anesthesiologist phoned the neonatal team as soon as he spotted me. Jackie was sitting on a stool at Carolyn's side. She was wearing scrubs, a surgical hat and a mask.

I walked over to Carolyn, and squeezed her shoulder.

"I'm here. We'll be starting in just a few minutes. Don't worry. Your baby will be delivered very quickly and the neonatologists will be taking over immediately."

She gave me a shaky smile. "Just promise me that everything will be okay."

"We'll all do our very best for you," I promised.

I left, went to the scrub sink, and did the usual five-minute surgical scrub. When I entered the operating room, the circulating nurse helped me to gown and glove.

The chief resident stood opposite me at the table. The scrub nurse handed me my purple marking pen. I drew a careful, symmetrical line on Carolyn's abdomen and reached for the scalpel, working my way down to the uterus. It seemed so small, compared to a full-term pregnancy.

The resident retracted the bladder out of the way, and I used my scalpel to make a careful uterine incision, taking it slowly, so I wouldn't risk cutting the baby. When I punctured the membranes, there was only a very small gush of clear amniotic fluid.

The baby was breech. I gently inserted my hand and guided the hips and legs out of the incision.

"You have a girl," I announced.

Once I'd delivered her, up to the waist, I wrapped her body in a towel to give me a better grip, and swept the arms down so I could deliver the chest.

The resident supported the tiny body as I reached for the head, slipping my finger into her mouth in order to flex the neck. The head delivered easily. I suctioned the mouth and nose, quickly cut the cord, and handed her to the neonatologist. She was the size of a kitten.

"Is she all right?" Carolyn asked

The baby gave a weak cry.

"She is and she's beautiful. They'll bring her over as soon as she's dry and warm. Have you decided on a name?" I asked.

"Sofia," Carolyn said.

I looked over at the neonatal team, and someone caught my eye and gave me the thumbs up.

I sighed with relief and began the process of delivering the placenta and sewing up.

When the surgery was over, I sat down at a computer terminal in the nursing station to enter orders and dictate my operative report. I'd keep Carolyn on anti-seizure medication for another twenty-four hours, but I didn't anticipate any trouble. Jackie had gone with baby Sophia to the NICU. I spotted her in the hallway, as I headed to my locker.

"Dr. Kline, thank you," she said. "That was the most amazing thing I've ever seen."

I smiled. "How is Sofia doing?"

"She's breathing on her own and is in an incubator. I can't get over how tiny she is. They weighed her, and she's only 850 grams. That's not even two pounds."

"I know," I said. "She's small, even for a premature baby, but she'll gain weight. I think they let the babies go home at three and a half pounds."

"When can I see Carolyn?" Jackie asked.

"You can go to the recovery room now if you like. She was doing just fine when I checked on her a few minutes ago. After you've had a few minutes to visit, why don't you go home and get some rest? Carolyn probably needs some sleep as well."

"That's not a bad idea. My own bed seems very tempting right now. See you tomorrow."

I wasn't sure that she would get any sleep. I suspected that Daniel would arrest her first.

CHAPTER FORTY-SEVEN

HANNAH MADE IT HOME, AS PROMISED, A LITTLE AFTER 4:00 a.m., and Daniel's cell rang about an hour later. He took the call in the hallway, so as not to disturb her badly needed sleep.

"Jackie just got home," the cop on duty said.

"Great. I'll get the team ready to search her house at 7:00 a.m. She's probably going straight to bed, but if she tries to leave before we get there in the morning, you need to detain her."

Daniel made the necessary calls and tiptoed back into the bedroom. He was too energized to sleep, but he could, at least, lie down and rest for another hour.

At a little after 6:00 a.m., Hannah rolled over, into his arms.

"Morning," she said. Her eyes were still closed.

"Barely morning," he said, and ran his hand over the curve of her body. It was hard to stay angry with her when she was so warm and voluptuous.

"Are you still mad at me?"

"Depends. Do you trust me?"

"With my life."

He smiled at her. "No, I'm not mad."

"Good. Me neither." She wrapped her leg around his hip and he moved his lips to her mouth.

"Do we have time for this?" he asked.

Let's make time," she said.

It wasn't their usual leisurely lovemaking, but it started the day on an improved note.

"How did your delivery go last night?" he asked her, as they stood in the bathroom, brushing their teeth.

She splashed warm water over her face and reached for a towel. "The baby was doing well when I left the hospital. She's amazingly small. It's going to be a long haul in the NICU."

"When can I talk to Carolyn?" he asked.

"Probably tomorrow or the next day. I can let you know when I discontinue the narcotics."

It was a peace offering and he accepted it as such.

"Thanks, honey. I have to go. I'll see you later."

"No breakfast?" Hannah asked.

"Brenda will probably show up with doughnuts," Daniel answered.

CHAPTER FORTY-EIGHT

DANIEL MET BRENDA, AND A VAN WITH FOUR OTHER police officers on Jackie's street. At this hour, the neighborhood was quiet. Brenda hadn't brought doughnuts, but she did hand him a cup of coffee.

"It's not poisoned," she said, grinning.

"Very funny," Daniel said. "Listen up everyone. Brenda is going to ring the doorbell and you four join us as soon as Jackie answers the door. I'll want Officer Perez to stay with her in the living room and watch her. Someone should search the powder room first, so that Jackie can use the facilities if necessary. Perez, you'll need to keep the bathroom door partly open, so she doesn't decide to lock herself in."

"What about the rest of us?" someone asked.

"Brenda and I will start searching the study and adjacent bathroom. I'd like you two guys to start on the master bedroom and bath, and you to search the kitchen. We're looking for any paper evidence that Jackie is J.C. Neuman, and any substance that might be the poison. I want you to confiscate everything you find in a powdered form, even if it looks like a box of talcum powder or salt. Everything goes to the lab," Daniel said.

"What about coffee grounds?" Brenda asked.

"Good idea. Grab the coffee, coffee bean grinder, anything coffee-related, just in case.

"Got it," Perez said.

Daniel and Brenda walked to the front door. Daniel stood to the side as Brenda rang the bell. She had to ring several times, and knock twice, before a voice answered through the intercom.

"Who's there?"

"Detective Brenda Jordan, Ms. Cantor. I need to talk to you. Please answer the door."

"Just a minute. I was asleep," Jackie said.

It was closer to five minutes before the door opened. Jackie clearly had been sleeping. She was barefoot, wearing a white terry cloth robe, and her ash blonde hair was disheveled.

"What's wrong?" she said.

"Ma'am, we have a search warrant for your home," Brenda said, handing Jackie the papers. "This is Detective Ross."

Jackie's eyes glanced briefly at Daniel and looked away. It was a good thing they'd never actually met.

"What is this about?" Jackie asked.

She was clearly coming awake, and she sounded angry.

"It's about the murder of your son-in-law, Edwin Larramore," Brenda said.

"What are you looking for?" Jackie asked.

"We'll let you know when we find it," Brenda said.

The police team entered the hallway, wearing shoe covers and gloves. Brenda escorted Jackie to the living room.

"We'd like you to wait here while we're searching," she

said. "Officer Perez will stay with you, in case you need anything."

Brenda motioned one of the officers to the powder room. Daniel nodded to the remaining team, and they headed off to find their assigned places.

Daniel and Brenda entered the study. He went immediately to the wall containing the diploma Hannah had found and removed it.

"Here's our first piece of evidence that we're in the right place," Daniel said, showing it to Brenda.

She nodded. She was at the bookcase, systematically removing books, checking inside and behind them. After a few minutes, she located Jackie's PhD thesis.

"Here's another piece," she said, flipping through it. "Jesus, look at the math in this thing. I barely made it though algebra. Jackie is way smart."

"Hopefully, not smart enough," Daniel said.

They bagged and labeled the two items. Brenda moved on to the desk, taking out drawers, checking underneath them, and examining all the files. Daniel opened the closet.

The closet was neat and orderly, and had been configured to hold office supplies. There were reams of paper, manila and white envelopes, file folders, staples and paper clips. On the floor were several cardboard file boxes. Daniel removed them, and placed them on the desktop to examine. Most of them seemed to contain files of completed old real estate deals, but there was one labeled Grad School.

The Grad School box contained a folder of reprints of the paper on Nickel Diarsine that J.C. Neuman had written. There was a larger folder labeled "Thesis Notes," filled with handwritten yellow papers, covered with mathematical calculations. Finally, there was a paper bag. Daniel opened it.

"What did you find?" Brenda asked.

Daniel removed two small glass containers, each about the size of a pill bottle. One contained several large blue crystals. The second was filled with a pale blue powder.

"I think I may have found the murder weapon," Daniel said. He reached for his cell phone and dialed Bill Pincus. "Bill, I think I've just found the elusive Nickel Diarsine. If I send a guy with the samples over to you right now, could you have the lab run it ASAP? I'm taking the suspect in for questioning, and it would be great to have a confirmation."

"I'll see what I can do," Bill said.

Brenda commandeered one of the officers, who was searching the bedroom, and Daniel sent him off with the carefully wrapped and labeled evidence. After the officer left, Brenda gave Daniel a high five.

The master suite search had netted lots of bathroom contents to be tested, but nothing else of significance. The kitchen had yielded primarily spices, Starbucks coffee beans, and a grinder. Daniel also confiscated Jackie's personal computer, her purse and phone, the thesis, diploma and the graduate school box. Then, he and Brenda proceeded to the living room.

"Ms. Cantor, we need to take you to the station for questioning. Officer Perez will go with you to your bedroom, while you dress, and she and I will escort you," Brenda said.

Brenda turned to Daniel, after they left the room. "What do you want to do next?"

"Let's leave two guys here to finish searching the house and garage, although I think we've got what we needed. I sent another team to Jackie's office to confiscate that computer, and see if there's anything else relevant."

Brenda nodded. "What about the lab?"

"You and I should search Carolyn's laboratory. We'll let Jackie stew down at the station, and question her when we're done."

"Are we going to the hospital to talk to Carolyn?" Brenda asked.

"Not until tomorrow," Daniel said. "She's on narcotic meds today. Nothing she says to us would be admissible in court."

Brenda nodded and reached for her handcuffs as Jackie, dressed neatly in a black sweater and tailored pants, her hair finally combed, came out of her bedroom, followed by Officer Perez.

"I don't think you'll need those to control a woman in her sixties," Daniel said. "Just lock her in the back seat of your police car."

"Ma'am," Brenda said, taking Jackie's arm. "Come with me please."

After Brenda's car pulled away, Daniel loaded the evidence from the study into the trunk of his car, and supervised while the remaining evidence was placed in the van. He and Brenda had agreed to meet at the station, and take one car to the Institute. Daniel wished they had been able to search Carolyn's lab earlier, but they hadn't had enough evidence to convince a judge to issue a warrant until now. The house had been a different story, as Edwin had lived there, and the home of a murder victim could always be searched for clues that would point in the direction of the killer.

As it turned out, the remaining searches of both the lab and Jackie's office yielded little of value. They took her laboratory computer to investigate her emails, and to see if, by any chance, she'd researched the poison.

It was late afternoon by the time they finished and stopped for some fast food. Daniel was anxious to get back to the station.

Jackie was in an interview room, pacing the floor. Officer Perez was watching her though a one-way mirror.

"How's she doing?" Daniel asked.

"She's pissed and agitated," Perez answered. "I've given her breakfast and lunch, and escorted her to the ladies room twice. She's demanding to know why she's here. I told her the detectives would be in and explain everything, as soon as the search is finished."

"Good," said Daniel. "People who are agitated are more likely to make mistakes when we interview them. Brenda, you take the lead. She knows you."

The two detectives walked in, Daniel carrying a recorder.

"Sorry it took so long," Brenda said. "Please, sit down. We're going to record this interview so that it can be transcribed and you can make sure it's accurate."

Daniel put the recorder on the table and turned it on. Brenda identified herself and Daniel, gave the date and time, and stated that this was an interview of Ms. Jacqueline Cantor.

"What the hell am I doing here?" Jackie asked.

"You're here because you're a suspect in the murder of your son-in-law, Edwin Larramore." Brenda read Jackie her rights. "Do you understand these rights, as I've read them to you?"

"Yes," she said. "But you're wrong, Detectives. I had nothing to do with Edwin's murder."

"Then you won't object to answering a few questions?" Brenda said.

Jackie stared at her.

"When we searched your study, we found a diploma from UCSD and a PhD thesis. Are you Jacqueline Cantor Neuman, also known as J.C.?" Brenda asked.

"I was J.C. Neuman. I divorced my husband a long time ago and resumed my maiden name," Jackie said.

"I'm a little puzzled about why an obviously brilliant woman, such as you, is selling real estate rather than doing scientific research. When did you give up chemistry?" Brenda asked.

"When I couldn't find a job," Jackie said. "There were very few academic jobs available at the time I was looking. There was a recession. Ronald Reagan had even instituted a tenure freeze at the University of California."

"Did you look for a job outside California?" Brenda asked.

"I looked in every metropolitan area all over the country. I was even invited to a few job interviews. Most department chairmen didn't figure out that J.C. Neuman was a woman, until I got there. Then it was crystal clear that I was the wrong gender. How is it at the LAPD, Detective Jordan? You think you get an even break as a female?"

Brenda ignored her questions. "So, how did you become a realtor?" she asked.

"My husband was a real estate developer. His father had a big construction company back East, and he wanted Robert to join him. When I couldn't find a decent job, we moved to Connecticut. I became pregnant with Carolyn, and eventually joined the family business. They taught me how to sell houses."

"Do you enjoy selling houses?"

"I make a hell of a lot more money in real estate than your average chemistry professor," Jackie said.

"You wrote your thesis on a compound called Nickel Diarsine," Brenda said. "Had you intended to continue researching it after graduate school?"

Jackie shrugged. "Maybe. There were still some unanswered questions. I never got the chance."

"Did you bring your leftover Nickel Diarsine with you when you left UCSD?" Brenda asked.

"I don't remember," Jackie said. "Why are you asking?"

It was time for "bad cop," Daniel thought. "Because," he said, "Nickel Diarsine was used to poison Edwin Larramore."

Jackie looked stunned. Either she was genuinely surprised or she was a very good actress.

"Did you poison your son-in-law?" Daniel asked.

"I'm not answering any more questions," Jackie said. "It's time to call my lawyer."

"Certainly," Brenda said. "We'll bring you a telephone."

She terminated the interview and Daniel shut off the recorder.

The two detectives left the room and Officer Perez came in with a portable phone. Daniel and Brenda watched through the mirror.

"I wish she hadn't opted for a lawyer so soon," Brenda said.

"As you pointed out, she's clearly a very smart woman. It was inevitable. I wonder if she thought the police labs were too incompetent to identify such an obscure chemical?" Daniel said.

Brenda shrugged. "I'm willing to bet that the sample you sent is the poison. With or without a confession, we've got enough to go to court."

"I hope so," Daniel said. "The only question is whether we're going to wind up arraigning Jackie or Carolyn."

CHAPTER FORTY-NINE

I GOT ZOE OFF TO SCHOOL AND MADE MORNING ROUNDS on Carolyn, who was doing well. Her blood pressure had come down, and she wasn't having much pain. I told the nurses to get her up and out of bed later that morning, and made a quick stop in the NICU for an update on baby Sophia. The baby was in an incubator and breathing on her own. She was much too small to nurse or suck on a nipple, so she was getting fed through a tiny tube, inserted down her throat to her stomach. Hopefully, Carolyn would be able to pump some breast milk in a day or two.

I was feeling exhausted after my interrupted night's sleep, so I drank two cups of coffee and dragged my way though my patient schedule. I made myself a mental note to stop and see Carolyn at the end of my day. I kept wondering what was happening with Jackie, but Daniel didn't call me, and I wasn't going to call him. Clearly, he wasn't angry anymore, but the sex hadn't solved the underlying issues between us, just swept them temporarily under the rug. As soon as his case was solved, we would have to confront what had happened.

I finished at my office a little after 4:00 p.m., and walked across the bridge to the hospital. I got Carolyn's chart, and took a quick look at the vital signs and the nurse's notes. Carolyn had gone twice to the NICU, in a wheelchair, to see her baby. I left orders to discontinue her IV and catheter in the morning, and to switch her to oral pain medication.

When I entered the room, Carolyn was in bed, and at first, I thought she was sleeping.

"Carolyn," I whispered.

She opened her eyes immediately. They looked puffy and bloodshot, as if she had been crying.

I pulled up a chair to the side of the bed. "Are you in pain?"

She shook her head. "It's my mother. They've arrested her."

"What?"

"Her attorney called me a little while ago. They think she murdered Edwin."

"Why would they think that?" I asked.

"They searched her house and found a chemical, apparently the same substance that was used to poison my husband."

Tears were rolling down her cheeks. I reached over and took her hand.

"Do they have proof that Jackie used it?" I asked.

"I don't know what they have. The lawyer told me it was a highly unusual chemical. The fact that Jackie had some in her house is very bad for her. The police think she killed Edwin to protect me. This is all my fault." Her shoulders began to shake. "I should never have told her that he was hitting me."

I let her cry it out on my shoulder. So, Jackie had been a

mother bear, I thought, just defending her cub from danger. Now, she would be punished for it.

"I'm so sorry, Carolyn. I can't imagine how difficult this is for you both. I know how close you are."

Carolyn reached for a tissue and wiped her eyes. "I always knew my mother loved me, but until I saw Sofia, I don't think I understood how much. I would throw myself in front of a train to protect my baby. I guess Mom felt the same way about me. God, I hate the police."

CHAPTER FIFTY

D ANIEL HAD WAITED PATIENTLY FOR JACKIE TO CALL her lawyer, who found her a criminal defense attorney. The two of them had a long meeting together. Daniel would need to continue questioning Jackie, with her attorney present, but he was content to wait until his lab results came back. He was only going to get one good shot at this and he wanted to make sure that all his ammunition was primed.

Bill Pincus called him that afternoon and confirmed both bottles had contained Nickel Diarsine. The lab called later, and told him the unidentified fingerprint on the coffee bag was Jackie's. Daniel was on a roll. But he needed to interview Carolyn.

Daniel and Brenda came together at the nursing station, later that afternoon. Daniel presented his police credentials to the charge nurse, and they were escorted to Carolyn's room. The nurse knocked and told Carolyn she had visitors.

Carolyn was sitting in bed, eating hospital food, or to be

more accurate, moving hospital food around on her plate with a fork. It looked very unappetizing.

"Oh, it's you," she said, when she saw Daniel. "I've been expecting you."

"We have a few questions, Dr. Larramore," Daniel said. "I assume you already know that your mother has been arrested in the murder of your husband."

She nodded, and reached over to her side table for an envelope. Opening it, she handed Daniel a card.

"This is the phone number of my attorney," she said. "I'm not talking to you without her being present. The two of you can decide on a time. I'll be here for several days, or so my doctor tells me."

"It's certainly your right to have an attorney present, Dr. Larramore," Daniel said. "But we aren't accusing you of anything. I'm not sure you need one."

"I'll be the judge of what I need, Detective," she said. "I know you bastards are trying to get me to say something that will help you send my mother to jail. Well, I won't. I want you to leave now."

"Congratulations on your new baby," Brenda said.

"Damn," Daniel said, as they waited for the hospital elevator. "That's what comes of waiting. Your witnesses get to prepare."

"We didn't have a choice. As you pointed out, we couldn't interview her while she was on a morphine drip. Obviously, Jackie made sure her lawyer told Carolyn what was going on, and recommended she get an attorney as well," Brenda said.

They took the elevator to the garage level. As Brenda

eased the car down the ramp to the street, Daniel's cell phone rang.

"Really?" he said. "No kidding. We'll be there in half-an-hour."

"Who was that?" Brenda asked.

"Izzy. Jackie is ready to make a statement. She wants to confess."

Jackie was waiting for them in the interview room. Her attorney, a tall, gray-haired man, wearing an Italian suit and a blue silk tie, sat next to her. Daniel and Brenda sat down, turned on the recorder and identified themselves and the two others in the room.

Daniel turned to Jackie. "I understand you wish to make a statement, Ms. Cantor."

Jackie nodded.

"For the record, and against my advice, my client has decided to confess to murdering her son-in-law, Edwin Larramore," the attorney said.

"Is that correct?" Daniel asked.

"It is," Jackie said. "I am responsible for Edwin's death."

"Can you tell us why you killed him?" Daniel asked.

"Edwin was abusing my daughter. During the years of their marriage, I observed many instances of verbal abuse, but a few months ago, I discovered that he was also beating her."

"Did you consider alternatives besides murder?" he asked. "For example, did you offer to help your daughter leave and get a divorce?"

"Carolyn was afraid to leave him. She would have had to change her name and hide in some other city. As long as she was employed at the Institute, there would have been no way to avoid him. Then, she became pregnant. Maybe she thought that becoming a father might change him. I knew better. I was afraid not only for my daughter, but for her child."

"How did you murder Edwin?" Daniel asked.

"You already know the answer to that. I put Nickel Diarsine in his espresso."

"I see. Why did you choose such an obscure chemical, Ms. Cantor? Or should I call you Doctor Cantor?" Daniel said.

"Because it was obscure, Detective. I suppose I didn't think the police would be able to identify it, let alone connect it to me. Besides it was the only poison I had around the house. You can't go into the local pharmacy and purchase rat poison containing arsenic these days."

"No, I don't suppose you can. I need a bit more detail, Dr. Cantor. Can you describe exactly how you went about adding the poison to the coffee? Did you enter his office when he wasn't there?"

"No. I knew Carolyn kept the coffee in the freezer. I stopped in at Peet's and bought a pound of espresso. Then, I emptied it into a bowl, put half a cup of it back in the bag, and mixed in the poison. Then, I refilled the bag, and exchanged it for one she had in the freezer."

"When did you do this?" Daniel asked.

"About a month before he died," Jackie said.

"Where was Carolyn when you made the exchange? Was she home?"

"No. I have a key to their house. I went during the day, when I knew they were both working. It wasn't difficult."

"You weren't afraid that your daughter might drink some of that coffee?" Brenda asked.

"My daughter was pregnant. She'd given up caffeine in favor of herbal tea."

"Did you take any precautions, to avoid leaving fingerprints?" Daniel asked.

Jackie nodded. "I wore latex gloves while I was working. At the end, I took a moist dish towel and wiped the bag."

"What did you do with the gloves and the bottle with the chemical?" Daniel asked.

"I put them in a paper bag, which I threw into an Institute trash can."

"Very thorough," Daniel said. "Did you plan this all by yourself, or did your daughter help you?"

"I didn't need any help, Detective. I'm a smart woman with a PhD. It doesn't take a team effort to add poison to a bag of coffee."

"Is there anything you want to add to your statement?" Daniel asked.

Jackie shook her head. Daniel noted the date and time again and signed off on the recording.

"We'll have this transcribed for your signature, Dr. Cantor. Then, you will be formally charged and there will be an arraignment. Your attorney will let you know what the process is."

Daniel shut off the recorder, and he and Brenda took it and left the room.

Brenda exhaled a deep breath. "Are you surprised?" she said.

"I don't buy it," Daniel said.

"Why not?" Brenda asked. "It seems consistent with

everything we know. We never released any information about the coffee."

"I think she's protecting Carolyn. Either Carolyn did it, and Jackie's surprise when we mentioned the Nickel Diarsine as the poison was genuine, or they did it together, and she's a good actress."

"Let's assume Carolyn did it independently," Brenda said. "Can we explain all the findings, as well as Jackie's confession?"

"I think so," Daniel said. "Carolyn's a chemist. She certainly would have known the subject of her mother's thesis and the fact that her mother had kept samples of Nickel Diarsine. It would have been easy for her to obtain some, and to mix it with the espresso in her own kitchen. Then, all she would have to do is dispose of the evidence and wait for Edwin to get to the bottom of the bag."

"How do we explain Jackie's fingerprint on the bag?" Brenda asked.

"She could have run an errand for her busy daughter, and picked up the coffee for her. Carolyn would have wiped the bag to get rid of all the fingerprints, but she didn't do it carefully enough."

"You still have to explain how Jackie could confess in such accurate detail, assuming she's innocent," Brenda said.

"Think it through, Brenda. Carolyn and her mother have been in constant communication since Edwin's death. Jackie must have asked a great many questions, and Carolyn could have told her that the police believed Edwin was poisoned by something in his coffee."

"How would Carolyn have known what we believed?" Brenda said.

"We asked her for details about Edwin's coffee when we broke the news of his homicide. We also told Jackie that

Nickel Diarsine was the poison. How hard could it be for a very smart woman to create a plausible scenario that kept the blame away from her daughter?"

"Okay, I agree," Brenda said. "Let's run through it again, assuming that they collaborated."

"That's easy," Daniel said. "Mother and daughter decide to poison the coffee. Carolyn buys it and Mom supplies the chemical. They mix it up together in Carolyn's kitchen, wipe the bag, get rid of the gloves and bottle. That's a much easier explanation for the fingerprints."

"Any suggestion on how to tell these two scenarios apart, and poke holes in Jackie's story?" Brenda asked.

"First of all, we should get Jackie's purse from the evidence room and see if she really has a key to Carolyn's house. Secondly, we should go through their credit card receipts and look for purchases at Peet's. I'd like to do that before we interview Carolyn."

"Good idea," Brenda said. "I don't know if you noticed, but Jackie buys her coffee at Starbucks."

CHAPTER FIFTY-ONE

I T WAS THREE DAYS AFTER THE CESAREAN SECTION when Daniel and Brenda returned to the hospital to interview Carolyn. She was obviously recovering well, because she was wearing makeup and a silk dressing gown. Her attorney, a middle-aged woman, was seated on a chair beside her bed. Carolyn made the introductions, and Daniel and Brenda shook hands. Then, Daniel placed a recorder on the side table and turned it on.

"Dr. Larramore, we are recording this interview so that it can be transcribed for your review and signature. We are questioning you as a witness in the murder of your husband, but just so there is no question of any legal impropriety, I am going to read you your rights."

"Clearly," Carolyn said, looking in the direction of her attorney, "I am quite aware of my rights."

"Dr. Larramore, you are no doubt aware that your mother has confessed to poisoning your husband. You, yourself, are a chemist. Were you familiar with the nature of your mother's chemical research?" he asked.

"Not in detail," she said. "My mother was a theoretical

and inorganic chemist. I'm a biochemist. Her work involved a level of mathematics beyond my abilities."

"Did you know she researched a chemical called Nickel Diarsine?" he asked.

Carolyn hesitated.

"Remember, you will be asked this question in court, under oath," Daniel said.

"Yes, I knew the name of the chemical she researched."

"Did you also know that your mother had some of that chemical at home?"

"I don't recall her ever mentioning it," Carolyn said.

"Did you and your mother help one another out, run errands for each other, for example?" Daniel asked.

"What kind of errands?"

"Oh, grocery shopping, picking up things at the cleaners?"

"Yes, occasionally," she said.

"Did your mother ever stop at Peet's for you, and pick up espresso for Edwin?"

"I don't remember."

"Did your husband abuse you, Dr. Larramore?" Carolyn glanced at her attorney, who nodded her head.

"Yes," she said.

"Did he hit you?"

"Yes."

"Did you tell your mother?" Daniel asked.

"She knew," Carolyn said. "She saw the bruises."

"Why didn't you leave him, Dr. Larramore?"

Carolyn buried her face in her hands for a moment, and then looked directly at Daniel.

"Because I was afraid of him, and because I was pregnant." she said.

"Did you and your mother have keys to one another's homes?" Daniel asked.

Carolyn glanced at her purse, which was on a chair in the corner. "I have a key to my mother's house. I lived with her until I graduated college."

"Does she have a key to your home?"

"No. Edwin refused to give anyone a key, or the alarm code, even Jackie."

"We'll need the key to your mother's home as evidence," Daniel said, taking out a plastic evidence bag. He handed the bag to the attorney, who retrieved the purse and gave it to Carolyn. Carolyn removed her key ring, took one of the keys from it, and dropped it in the bag. The attorney passed the bag to Daniel.

"Thank you," he said. "I have another question. Did you collaborate with your mother to murder your husband?"

"Don't answer that question," the attorney said.

"Let me put it another way," said Daniel. "Can you explain to me how your mother could have put poison in Edwin's coffee supply if she didn't have access to your house?"

"I don't believe, for a moment, that my mother did this," Carolyn said. "Are we done?"

"For now," Daniel said.

"I think you're correct," Brenda said. "Jackie's confession isn't holding up. There's no key to the Larramore's home in her purse. There's also no credit card purchase at Peet's within three months of Larramore's murder, but she routinely used her credit card when purchasing coffee at

Starbucks. She couldn't have committed the murder the way she claimed she did."

"The scenario that fits the evidence best is a collaborative effort. I wonder if Carolyn's fingerprints are anywhere on the bottles with the poison." Daniel said.

Brenda shook her head. "They aren't. I checked this morning. Jackie's are, but you'd expect them to be. This brings up another question. Why didn't Jackie get rid of the poison? If she used and disposed of one bottle, why keep the others at home?"

"Hubris," Daniel said. "She probably figured the police were too dumb to trace it to her."

"Well, I guess we weren't too dumb, were we?" Brenda said.

"Don't get too confident," Daniel said. "We've undermined Jackie's confession, but we don't have a shred of real evidence linking the poison to Carolyn. If Jackie confessed to protect her daughter, she'll probably succeed. Either way," Daniel sighed, "Hannah and I are going to need a new realtor."

CHAPTER FIFTY-TWO

I HAD MADE ROUNDS ON CAROLYN EARLY IN THE morning, so I knew that Jackie had confessed and that Daniel was coming to the hospital later in the day. I could only think of one reason he would want to interview Carolyn. He must suspect her of being an accessory, if not an equal partner in the murder. I hoped he was wrong. I wanted this whole thing to be over.

I made light conversation with Daniel all through dinner, and then the three of us watched the Disney channel until it was time for Zoe to go bed. I joined him downstairs after I'd tucked her in.

"Carolyn told me that Jackie confessed to the murder," I said. "Does that mean it's over?"

Daniel hesitated. "I don't know yet. That depends on whether the prosecuting attorney is satisfied with her statement."

"I guess I'm not as good a judge of character as I thought I was," I said. "I'd never have imagined Jackie as a murderer in a million years."

"That's the problem with killers. They often look like the most ordinary people," he said.

"Are you satisfied that your case is solved?" I asked.

He didn't answer. That was answer enough.

"You still think Carolyn played a part, don't you?"

"I can't discuss it," he said.

The tragic thing was that he was probably right. I could hear Carolyn's voice in my head, saying, "Mom and I have been a team since I was four years old. There's nothing we wouldn't do for one another."

I wondered if Daniel would be able to find enough evidence to prove her guilt. I hoped not.

"You know, it was nice making love this morning, and it made both of us less angry, but it just put a Band-Aid over the real issues. I've never seen you lose your temper like that, before."

Daniel sighed. "I know. I'm sorry. I just...I never felt like you didn't trust me, before."

"I'm sorry. I do trust you. But I felt like I was being shut out. You were more than happy to have my help on previous cases, when I had an inside track. Why was I suddenly persona non grata in this case? Do you think I enjoy it when people I know are murdered?"

Daniel's brow furrowed and he waited awhile before speaking. I could tell he was weighing his words.

"Hannah, you are the smartest person I know. When you've been able to help me with your insights, your intelligence, and your inside access, I've been very appreciative. But I hate it when you put yourself at risk. You've had two close calls because what you knew was threatening to a killer. It would be unbearable to me if anything happened to you, because you were trying to help me solve a case." His voice broke.

"I had no idea you were so worried about me," I said. "I worry about you too. You're at risk much more often than I am."

"That's true, but I'm trained for it, I'm armed, and it's my job."

"Maybe we'll luck out," I said. "And bad things will stop happening to people we know."

"That would be nice," Daniel said. "But just in case something comes up, can we make a deal?"

"What kind of a deal?" I asked.

"Anytime you think you can help me, we plan it together ahead of time. And if I think it's too dangerous, you don't do it."

"Sounds fair," I said. "I'm honestly not a risk taker. I'm the mother of a six-year-old, and I do think before I act, but I understand where you're coming from. And I have no problem with it."

"So, we're agreed?"

I got up from my chair and walked toward him.

"Sealed with a kiss," I said.

The next morning, I discharged Carolyn from the hospital. Oliver came to take her home, and volunteered to be her chauffeur until I gave her post-op permission to drive. I imagined she would be making daily trips to the NICU, and frequent visits to the jail.

"What's going to happen to Jackie?" I asked Daniel, a few weeks later. As far as the LAPD was concerned the investigation was over. Daniel had turned over all his findings to the prosecuting attorney and been assigned a new case. Apparently, it was now okay for him to talk about it with me.

"That's partly up to her," he said. "She was charged with first degree murder at the arraignment and pled not guilty. The prosecuting attorney might offer her a deal, if she pleads guilty, or he might choose to go to trial and offer nothing. It's a high-profile case, and Jackie's fingerprint on the coffee bag, as well as the poison found in her home, gives him a good deal of ammunition. On the other hand, I found several holes in her confession that the defense attorney could use. False confessions are common, and the jury might be very sympathetic to Jackie. She's a loving mother, defending her daughter and grandchild. A good attorney might get her off."

"What about Carolyn?" I asked.

"I truly believe that the death of Edwin Larramore was a joint project," Daniel said. "But there simply isn't any forensic evidence that ties her to the murder. The only way she could be charged is if Jackie testified against her."

"I can't believe that would ever happen," I said.

"I can't either," he said. "The biggest frustration in my job is that sometimes, no matter how hard I try, I can't tie up all the loose ends."

I smiled and put my arms around him. "That's because people are complicated, and nothing is ever purely black or white. All you can do is your best. I've never seen you do anything less."

EPILOGUE
THREE MONTHS LATER

D ANIEL AND I FOUND A NEW REALTOR, ONE WITH NO connection to Jackie, to any of my patients, or to his ex-wife, Annie. We spent a good many weekends in fruitless house hunting. Then, one evening, we were blessed by the Gods of Real Estate. Our realtor called us.

"Remember that house, off Kenter Canyon, that you said you'd liked, but missed out on, because it sold?"

I'd mentioned the house without telling the whole story, but it had been the fantasy in the back of my mind as we had hunted.

"I remember," I said. "What about it?"

"It just fell out of escrow. Do you want to make an offer?"

We did, and it was accepted. I set about hiring a contractor to remodel the kitchen and bathrooms. We replaced the orange carpet, and Zoe picked out the colors for her rooms. As soon as we were ready to move, I would put my condominium on the market.

～

I saw Carolyn in my office for her six-week postpartum visit. She'd brought Oliver Wilson with her, and he seemed very attentive. Just last week, baby Sofia had been discharged from the NICU, without any major medical issues. I'd taken a deep breath of relief.

Jackie was in jail, awaiting trial. It remained to be seen whether the prosecution or the defense would prevail. Either way, Daniel seemed resigned to the outcome.

We were at the new house, checking on the remodel. I stepped out onto the deck and admired the lovely view over the canyon. Daniel came up behind me, and put his arms around my waist.

"I have a thought," I said, turning into his embrace. "Wouldn't this deck be the absolutely perfect place for a small, intimate wedding?"

He gave me a huge smile and tightened his hug. "Outstanding idea," he said.

We sealed that bargain with another kiss.

ACKNOWLEDGMENTS

A number of people contributed to this novel and deserve my thanks.

First and foremost, my editor Linda Schreyer, whose wisdom and unfailing instinct for a good story line has been invaluable. My fellow writing student, Cathy Novak, has given me loads of insightful feedback.

Special thanks to Dr. Bruce Peterson, world class astronomer and old friend, who allowed me to pick his brain about the world of academic astronomy and the search for extrasolar planets.

Defense attorney Jerry Bernstein made certain I didn't make legal mistakes, and Ann Berlstein was my source of information for what goes on in the first grade.

My publisher, Christiana Miller, was responsible for the copy edits and formatting, and Kristin Bryant, our new designer, created the cover.

My husband Uri is always my first reader and IT expert, and I rely on him to make sure I haven't violated any laws of physics. Thank you all. I couldn't have written this without you.

Paula Bernstein is a New York native, who migrated to LA to attend graduate school in Chemistry. She acquired a PhD, an exceptionally nice husband, and the ability to synthesize creative meals from leftovers. Not long afterwards, she escaped her laboratory and attended medical school.

Like her series heroine, Hannah Kline, Paula spent her professional life practicing Obstetrics and Gynecology. When she developed an irresistible desire for an uninterrupted nights' sleep, she retired from her full time practice, and reinvented herself as a writer of medical mysteries.

Learn more about her at her website: https://www.hannahklinemysteries.com/

www.ingramcontent.com/pod-product-compliance
Lightning Source LLC
Chambersburg PA
CBHW031122160726
47989CB00016B/117